Oceans Beneath

Maiden to the Dragon, Book 5

Mac Flynn

All names, places, and events depicted in this book are fictional and products of the author's imagination.

No part of this publication may be reproduced, stored in a retrieval system, converted to another format, or transmitted in any form without explicit, written permission from the publisher of this work. For information regarding redistribution or to contact the author, write to the publisher at the following address.

Crescent Moon Studios, Inc.
P.O. Box 117
Riverside, WA 98849

Website: www.macflynn.com
Email: mac@macflynn.com

ISBN / EAN-13: 9781791893170

Copyright © 2018 by Mac Flynn

First Edition

CONTENTS

Chapter 1..1
Chapter 2..9
Chapter 3...16
Chapter 4...22
Chapter 5...30
Chapter 6...36
Chapter 7...43
Chapter 8...49
Chapter 9...55
Chapter 10...64
Chapter 11...71
Chapter 12...79
Chapter 13...86
Chapter 14...95
Chapter 15..102
Chapter 16..108
Chapter 17..115
Chapter 18..122
Chapter 19..131
Chapter 20..137
Chapter 21..145
Chapter 22..152
Chapter 23..160
Chapter 24..167
Chapter 25..175
Chapter 26..182
Chapter 27..186
Chapter 28..192

Continue the adventure......................................199
Other series by Mac Flynn.................................206

OCEANS BENEATH DRAGONS

CHAPTER 1

I lifted my chin in the air and closed my eyes. The sweet smell of salt air hit my nostrils and tingled my senses. I wrinkled my nose and let out a soft sneeze.

"Find peace," Xander spoke up.

I glanced to my left where my dragon lord rode beside me. Behind us was a short caravan of guards and Captain Spiros. The scenery around us was one of green beauty. Well-spaced trees cooled us with their branches and soft tufts of grass eased the trot of our horses as we traveled along a flat, wide trail. Sunlight lit up patches of the forest, and here and there hung thick vines. A few birds sat in the branches and sang their cooing songs to us.

I arched an eyebrow at Xander. "I might be able to find peace here, but these bugs have got to go." I winced and slapped my neck. A miss.

He smiled. "It is an old phrase that blesses you and keeps the demons from inhabiting the space just vacated by your sneeze."

My eyes widened. "Ooh, right. Like saying 'gesundheit.'"

It was his turn to give me a blank expression. "I do not know that phrase. Is it from a different language than your own?"

I nodded. "Yeah, it's German."

"And that is not your own?" he wondered.

I shook my head. "No. I speak English." I paused and furrowed my brow. "Now that I think of it, everyone in this world seems to speak my language."

Xander nodded. "Yes. The Portal has granted us constant communication to your world. Where the sus have lacked in their transference of culture, the Maidens have provided."

"What do the Maidens have to do with language?" I asked him.

Spiros eased up along my right side. "The Maidens, though captured like slaves, have always been held in high esteem by the nobility. They in turn have mimicked the Maidens' language, and that was then passed down to the people."

"Huh. Language is a funny thing," I commented. A sharp pain in my neck made me wince and slap the spot. A soft 'splat' noise told me I was successful. I drew my hand away and stuck out my tongue when I saw the sticky substance of bug goop on my palm. I wiped the muck on my jeans and glanced at Xander. "You know what's not funny is all these bugs. Are we almost out of this sweltering jungle?"

OCEANS BENEATH DRAGONS

Xander stood on his stirrups and looked ahead of us without stopping. A small smile curled onto his lips. "I believe your wish has been granted."

I mimicked his movements and watched our destination come into view. The trees parted and opened into a long field that stretched for five miles. In those miles was tall, wheat-like grass that waved in the salty breeze. Small stones houses with thatched roof dotted the landscape, and low stone walls bordered the road and divided the grass-rich plains into small squares. Sheep, cows, horses, and a few other beasts I didn't recognize roamed among the stone walls chewing on the wealth of grass. Little country lanes connected the houses, and on either side of their picturesque dirt paths were tall, elegantly cut trees.

At the end of the five miles the greenery was slowly transformed into beach. Pockets of white sand mixed with the grass until there was pockets of beach grass mixed with the sand. Beyond the white lay a vast expanse of blue-green water that twinkled in the dimming daylight.

I took in the view and found myself breathless. "Wow. . ." I murmured.

Xander smiled. "Cayden will be pleased with your response."

I plopped back down onto my saddle and returned my attention to Xander. "Can all dragon lords afford to have a home on the beach like Cayden?"

"Our ancient lines do denote a certain amount of wealth, but some of us were more fortunate with the lands we inherited," he admitted as he swept his eyes over the scenery. "Cayden was fortunate to inherit the southeastern coast with its wealth of beaches and farmland."

A teasing smile slipped onto my lips. "So you're saying you don't have one?"

Xander pursed his lips and shifted in his saddle. "Not at the present, no."

I grinned and looked ahead. "So when are Cayden and Stephanie supposed to meet us here?"

"Lord Cayden will be here in a day or two. He was delayed with certain problems along the coast south of here," Spiros told me.

Xander glanced at his captain. "Have you heard what comprised these problems?"

Spiros nodded. "I have heard that a crude tribe of humans have been raiding the coastline. They take the animals from the fields and drive them onto their ships."

Xander raised an eyebrow. "But they do not take the wheat from the granaries?"

Spiros shook his head. "No."

My dragon lord pursed his lips. "That is very unusual."

"Why is it unusual?" I spoke up. "Maybe they don't like grains."

"Grains are easier to take away, particularly on ships, and grains are more difficult to grow on the islands they inhabit," he pointed out.

I tightened my grip on the reins and looked ahead. "Well, I'm not going to let a couple of raids spoil my vacation."

I kicked my heels against the sides of my horse and spurred the steed into a fast gallop. The wind whipped at my long hair as the others in our group hurried after me. The nose on Xander's horse matched mine and exceeded it.

I grinned and ducked low in the saddle. "I'm not going to let you win that easily."

OCEANS BENEATH DRAGONS

A quick kick and my horse leapt into an all-out sprint. The world flew by in hues of green and blue. The hooves of my stead pounded the hard grass in quick beats. I laughed as the horse's mane brushed against my face.

Xander came up beside me and we burst into the field area together. We came up to one of the thatched cottages. A short wall surrounded the yard, and a small gate led from the yard onto the road. The gate swung open and a small boy with short wings on his back rushed into the road.

My eyes widened. I drew back and yanked on the reins. The horse whinnied and slid to a stop a few feet short of the boy. I didn't. Motion propelled me over the horn of the saddle and onto the road between the boy and my horse. I landed hard on my rear and winced as a sharp pain ran up my spine.

Xander stopped before I did and leapt down. He rushed over and knelt beside me. "Are you unhurt?"

I sat up and nodded. "Everything but my pride." I glanced over at the boy. He couldn't have been more than five and stared at us with wide eyes. "You should watch where you're going, kid."

"Colin? Colin, where are you?" a female voice cried out. A woman flew from the house and saw us on the other side of the wall. Her face turned ashen and she picked up her dress before she rushed over to us. "What's happened? Where's my-" She reached the gate and her eyes fell on the little boy. Her eyebrows crashed down. She put her hands on her hips and glared down at the young lad. "Colin, what in the world have you done now?"

His wings quivered as he shook his head. "Nothing, Mother, I swear it! I was only going out into the road to see what was all the commotion-"

"And you ran right out without looking again, didn't you?" she scolded him.

"It's all right," I spoke up as Xander helped me to my feet. I smiled at mother and son. "I shouldn't have been riding that fast, anyway."

The woman swept her eyes over our little caravan. Her attention stopped on the cloaks worn by the guards, and the symbol of Xander's house that peeked out from the clothing. She clasped her hands in front of herself and bowed her head. "I am truly sorry, Your Lordship. He's a naughty child who-"

"It's quite all right," Xander assured her. He knelt down in front of the lad who turned to face him. "How old are you?"

The lad perked up and stood as tall as his three-foot height would allow him. "I'll be six come this harvest."

Xander smiled and reached into his cloak. He drew out a small wooden whistle. "Then here is an early present for you."

The boy's face lit up as he took the gift. "Really? All for me?"

"Only if you promise to whistle before you run out into the road," Xander told him.

Colin nodded. "I will! I promise!"

"Then it is yours."

Xander handed Colin the little toy. The boy put the mouth of the whistle to his lips and blew. Its shrill call echoed over the road and yard. He lifted his head and grinned at Xander. "I bet I can get the whole of the beach to hear this! Especially from the cliffs!"

"What do you say to the kind lord?" his mother scolded him.

Colin bowed his head. "Thank you so much!" He ran off down the road.

"Don't go off to the beach! We'll go there tomorrow!" his mother called after him.

Xander stood and looked to the woman. "He is a fine boy."

His mother watched him and shook her head as a small smile danced across her lips. "Yes, and so much like his father." She returned her attention to us and bowed her head. "I do apologize for the trouble, Your Lordship, and thank you very much for the gift."

Xander shook his head. "There was no trouble, and I can procure more of whistles."

"But it was still very good of you to do that for my little boy," she persisted.

"My Lord, there is still a ways for us to travel," Spiros spoke up.

The woman gasped and stepped back into her yard. "I beg your pardon, My Lord. I won't keep you any longer." She bowed one last time before she hurried into the house.

Xander turned away from the scene and climbed into his saddle. "Where did you get the whistle?" I asked him as I mounted my steed.

He grabbed his reins and turned his horse toward the beach. "I crafted it."

I stared at him as he trotted past me. "You crafted it? Like you made it?"

Spiros came up beside me and there was a teasing smile on his lips. "Our Lord is quite the whittler, though he denies it. So great was his love of carving that his father once suggested he be apprenticed to a carpenter."

Xander stopped his horse and looked over his shoulder at us. "Will you talk all day there or may we continue on?"

Spiros grinned and bowed his head. "Whatever you say, My Lord Whittler." I snorted as we trotted down the road to our nice, long, relaxing vacation.

If only it had turned out that way.

CHAPTER 2

Our horses carried us down the road to where the grass met the sand. The road split left and right and followed the short hill a few miles in both directions. We stopped at the top of the gentle slope and enjoyed the salty breeze as it wafted over us. It carried with it a promise of fun and relaxation. There was also a hint of nightfall in its scent as the sun lowered itself below the horizon.

The sand sloped downward to the edges of the green-blue water that stretched beyond my sight. A few docks stretched from halfway along the beach far out into the water. Small sailing vessels were anchored at their posts and rocked gently on the water. Two lines of short white cliffs some one five miles apart stretched out into the water. They moved toward each other in long arcs that came close together two miles out. An opening three hundred feet wide allowed water into the area and created a large, calm bay. Around the wide mouth of the bay were dark shadows in the water that hinted at reefs.

Atop the right-hand, or southerly, cliff was a long, low stone dwelling. A half dozen rock-walled chateaus stood between the edge of grass and sand. Their foundations were carved from shell-covered gray boulders that lay scattered along the shoreline, remnants of an ancient cliff that was eroded before its brethren. They looked out on the smooth, sandy beach like guards of old.

I looked up and down the beach at the half dozen chateaus. "So which one belongs to Cayden?"

Xander nodded at a chateau some two hundred feet to our left. The large stones that made up the walls were smoothed by countless ocean breezes. Dark, weathered wood frames around the tall, latticed windows reminded one of elegant driftwood. A stone patio sat on the beach side of the structure and looked out on the calm waters. Stone steps led from the patio down to the beach, and a sturdy dock stretched out into the waters.

I glanced back to Xander. "Think he'll let me keep it?"

Xander smiled and turned his horse in the direction of our temporary quarters. "That is not likely. The home has been in his family for ten generations."

I scoffed. "That's not that long."

Spiros came up beside me. "The generation of a dragon is two hundred years."

I whistled as we trotted down the beach road. "Now *that's* a lot of math, but maybe he'll let me build a quaint shack nearby. Something with ten bedrooms."

We reached the short road that led up to the double doors that made up the front entrance. The doors opened and Darda stepped out. She smiled and bowed to us as we rode up and dismounted.

"I hope your journey was uneventful," she greeted us.

"It was until I decided I was a jockey and almost ran over a little boy," I commented.

Her eyes widened. "Was anyone hurt?"

I shook my head as I handed my reins to one of the guards. "No, but remind me to stop showing off when I have no idea what I'm doing."

Darda smiled and bowed her head. "I will do as you wish, but I may find your command very time-consuming."

Xander arched an eyebrow and his eyes flickered to Spiros. "Your insubordination appears to be contagious."

Spiros laughed as we four went inside. "I will take the credit for *this* illness."

I glanced from one to the other. "I'm guessing there's a story behind that remark."

Spiros nodded. "Yes. Our Lord happened to catch a very dire case of dragon pox and insisted I had somehow knowingly given it to him."

"You escaped from your sick bed to show me the spots," Xander reminded him.

Spiros furrowed his brow and shook his head, but his eyes twinkled with mischief. "I cannot recall that part. Perhaps the illness wiped my memories."

As they went back and forth in their game of denial and insistence, I stopped and looked around. The foyer of the house was two floors and spacious, but simple. A door on either side led to the wings of the building, and a hallway led straight through to the rear door.

I jumped when an arm slipped around mine and looked to see Darda by my side. She smiled at me and nodded at the rear door. "Would you like to see the view, Miriam?"

I smiled and nodded. "Very much."

We left the bickering men and walked past the whitewashed walls to the double-doors. Darda opened one, and I stepped out. A sea breeze greeted me, along with an amazing view of the bay. I walked to the stone railing and looked out. The green-blue water was so clear I could see the fish swimming through short bands of seaweed some two hundred feet out. The cliffs blocked much of the view beyond their walls, but I glimpsed a few dots of land on the horizon.

"It is quite a sight, is it not?" Darda asked me.

I leaned my arms against the top of the railing and smiled. "Yeah. I think I could live here forever."

"I would not be pleased with such an arrangement," Xander commented as he came up to my other side. He glanced over me at Darda. "Have all the preparations been finished?"

Darda bowed her head. "They have, My Lord, and we received a message from Lord Cayden that he and his Maiden are to arrive tomorrow at midday."

I looked to Xander. "What preparations?"

He leaned his side against the railing and smiled down at me. "I thought perhaps you would wish to test the waters here with your fishing as you did in Alexandria."

I straightened and rubbed my hands together. "Now you're speaking my language, but I'll do it only if I don't have to cook them. Or gut them."

"Or catch them?" he teased.

I snorted and shrugged. "I might not be doing much of that, either. Beriadan kind of helped me at the lake."

Xander pushed off the railing and offered me his arm. "Then we shall see your true skills, but for now let us-" A loud, long wail wrapped around us.

I clapped my hands over my ears and glanced up at Xander. "More ghosts?"

Xander pursed his lips and glanced down the beach. "No. That is the warning call."

I rose my voice to a shout to be heard above the terrible wail. "THEN WHY DOES IT SOUND LIKE THAT-" the siren cut off, "-CRY OF THE TRAITOR?" I cringed and lowered my hands. "Sorry."

Spiros hurried through the doors and onto the patio. "Xander, the light around the barracks are lit."

Xander turned to his captain. "Then we will find out what is the matter."

I wrapped my arm around his. "Yes, we will."

He paused and looked down at me. "I would rather you-"

"-stayed here, but we both know that's not going to happen, so let's go already," I insisted as I dragged him toward the door.

Spiros stood in the way. He smiled and gestured to the stone steps to his right that led down to the beach. "The barracks are this way."

"Oh. Right. I was going to know that." I turned Xander and myself toward the steps and marched down them.

Spiros and Darda followed, and I let Xander lead me reluctantly across the crunchy sand. He set his hand on mine and glanced down at me. "I would rather you had stayed behind. We do not know what danger lies ahead."

I nodded. "I know, but since I always seem to find the danger anyway I thought I'd better come with you."

He looked ahead and a small, crooked smile teased the corners of his lips. "I must admit you have a certain knack for finding trouble."

"It's a gift, now tell me about this barracks and why that noise sounded like a banshee," I insisted.

Xander chuckled. "Because the siren was meant to mimic the cry of the banshee."

I tilted my head to one side and gave him a side glance. "Seriously?"

He nodded. "Very seriously. The people of Cayden's realm have a great many stories of the banshee, a creature native to their dark forests and rocky coasts."

"Do any of those stories have to do with imminent death?" I wondered.

"A great many, but the warning call will not harm us. It is only a shadow of the true cry," he assured me.

I raised an eyebrow. "So why did they make their warning sound like that? And what are they warning us about?"

"Did you notice the siren?" he asked me.

I shivered and nodded. "Yeah, why?"

"A warning call that is not heard is worse than useless. It gives those in its influence a false state of security," he explained. He glanced at the coast line and the rocky cliffs that jutted out into the ocean. "A banshee's call is very efficient at traveling over great distances, so it creates a very useful warning call."

"And why they warned us in the first place?"

OCEANS BENEATH DRAGONS

His eyes settled on the long, low building of stone. "That is what we will find out."

We reached the end of the beach and found a staircase carved into the stones of the cliff. It gently arced to our left and reached the top of the cliff. We followed the stairs and walked across the flat surface. The cliff dropped off on either side of us. The left was the calm waters of the bay, and on the right was a rocky mess of sandy mud covered in bunches of seaweed. The shore stretched into the forest that surrounded the tiny valley, and civilization disappeared for miles beyond that.

A few large stones dotted the path on either side of us, but otherwise the way was clear up to the stone building. The roof was made up of terracotta tiles, and a few square windows ran along both sides. A single door in the center of the short end of the building led inside. The entrance was open, and around the exterior were men in gold-tinted armor.

One of them wore a helmet with a tall plume sticking out of the top. He glanced in our direction and raised one gloved hand toward us. "Halt!"

CHAPTER 3

We stopped and a half dozen of the guards, all with long halberds, hurried over to us with the plumed helmet fellow in the lead. The soldiers grouped themselves into an arc and pointed the tips of their weapons at us. He stopped before us and looked over our group. "Please state your business here."

"We came to investigate the call," Xander spoke up.

The man shook his helmeted head. "There is no cause for concern, sir. The alarm was proven to be false."

Xander looked around at the halberd-wielding men. Some of their points shook. "There appears to be cause for concern among your soldiers, captain. May I ask what is the matter?"

The man straightened and frowned. "That is something you need not concern yourself with, sir."

"Lord Cayden may not be of the same mind," Xander returned.

The captain's face blanched. "L-Lord Cayden? What has he to do with this?"

Xander swept his gaze over the others who were equally nervous. "He is coming tomorrow to entertain us at his home."

Their leader stiffened and his eyes widened. "T-then you are-?"

"Lord Xander," Xander finished for him.

The guards stepped back and glanced at one another. The captain swallowed a lump in his throat the size of an ostrich egg before he bowed his head. "My sincerest apologies, Your Lordship. If we had any idea-" He raised his head and found the others still pointed the tips of their weapons at us. He glared at him. "At attention, you fools! You point your weapons at Ferus Draco!" They stood at attention so quickly that half of them banged their metal halberds against their metal armor.

Xander held up his hand. "That is quite all right. We approached without introducing ourselves, but I wonder at your concern. Is something amiss?"

The captain pursed his lips. "I do not know if you have heard, Your Lordship, but humans have raided much of our coastline. It may only be a matter of time before they wish to take away our livestock as they did the others. It was they who our sentry thought they witnessed on the waters."

"What was it they saw?" Xander asked him.

The captain smiled. "Only a mess of drifting seaweed, Your Lordship."

Spiros stepped forward. "To where did the seaweed float?"

The captain shook his head. "I do not know. The tide might have taken it back out to sea or around the cliffs."

Spiros glanced at Xander who shook his head before he turned his attention to the captain. He bowed to him. "Thank you for being so forthcoming, captain. We are much obliged for the information."

The captain returned the bow. "It was a pleasure to meet you, Lord Xander, and might you tell Our Lord that he is very welcome to visit us when he arrives."

"I will pass on the message, and I am sure he will be pleased to oblige you," Xander promised.

We parted company and walked back to the stairs. I glanced between Xander's pensive look and Spiros's tense expression. "Well? What's up?"

Xander looked to his own captain. "You doubt the seaweed is as harmless as the captain professes?"

Spiros stopped us at the steps and grasped the hilt of his sword before he nodded. "I do. If you will recall Captain Magnus used much the same device to spy on our own ships before the battle."

"Hiding in seaweed?" I spoke up.

Xander cupped his chin in his hand and furrowed his brow. "I had forgotten that trick, but you are correct. Raiders may use the same tactic to inspect the coast prior to attacking, and because of that we must be wary."

My shoulders slumped and my face fell. "So does that mean the vacation is off?"

Xander dropped his hand and smiled at me. "Far from it. We can only speculate what may come, but unless they attack our conversation means nothing."

"What's going on up there?" an aged, raspy voice spoke up.

OCEANS BENEATH DRAGONS

We all looked down the stairs and watched a weathered man of seventy. His skin was browned and stretched like leather, and on his head was a worn cap. He wore a patched blue-and-gray overcoat over his coveralls and gray shirt, and on his feet were black boots that clomped against the steps. His faded blue pants were kept up with suspenders.

He reached us and studied each member of our group with a quick eye. "Well? Have the fish snapped your tongues off?" His wandering gaze stopped on Xander and his eyes widened. A crooked smile curled onto his lips. "Well, I'll be married to a fae."

Xander smiled at him. "According to some of your stories, you were."

The man laughed and clapped one of Xander's hands in both of his own. "Then I'll be leaving those stories out when I get you beside the campfire, but what good winds brought you back to these shores, My Lord?"

Xander gave his hands a hearty shake. "A need for rest and fun, and perhaps a few tales of the old days. Do you still tell your tall tales around the fires on the beach?"

The man nodded. "Aye, for any who are willing to hear them. Nowadays, that's the young ones hereabouts."

"Then I shall be young again, and I bring you one still younger." Xander nodded at me. "Dreail, allow me to introduce you to my Maiden, Miriam. Miriam, this is Captain Dreail, a teller of tale tales-"

"Some of them are true," Dreail argued.

Xander smiled and bowed his head. "A teller of tales and a man so of the sea the gods should have fated him to be a Mare fae."

Dreail eyed me with a studious stare before his attention flickered back to Xander. "You've caught yourself an interesting fish, My Lord. I haven't seen the likes of her for a great many years."

"Then you recognize her as a Mare?" Xander guessed.

He looked back to me and nodded. "Aye, but a halfling, isn't she?"

My heart quickened. "So I'm really a half Mare fae?"

He nodded. "Aye, I can see it in your eyes. There's something not quite right about them. Reminds me of the shadows in the deepest waters, but with a blemish of sorts. Sort of if a boat ran through the water and kind of wrecked the look of it."

"Can you give us any clues to her fae origins?" Xander asked him.

The old sea dog shook his head. "Nope. I can just see what she is, not who she belongs to."

My heart fell along with my shoulders. "Damn. . ."

Xander pursed his lips at me before he returned his attention to the captain. "Would you oblige us this night by regaling us with your tales? They would be new to many of us, and a second treat for myself."

The captain perked up and grinned. "I would be delighted, My Lord. Does anything suit your fancy?"

Xander looked over his shoulder at the guard barracks. "What of the tales of the banshee? Those seem rather appropriate considering this evening's call."

Dreail nodded. "Aye, a good choice, My Lord. I shall scrounge up my old tales and meet you above your dock at the usual hour."

Xander bowed his head. "We look forward to it."

The old captain turned and clomped down the stairs. I looked up at Xander. "What's the usual hour?"

Xander slyly smiled at me. "Midnight."

My face fell. "Seriously?"

He chuckled. "You doubt my word quite often, my Maiden."

I smiled. "I guess I have a hard time believing we're going to be sitting on a beach at midnight telling tall tales." I snorted and shook my head. "With me not being a part of this world I doubt I'll be able to tell what's tall and what's not."

His smile softened as he shook his head. "You are a fae, and they are as part of this world as any dragon. Perhaps more so." He half turned away. "But come. Let us return to the house before night sets in."

I walked a few steps, but paused and looked out on the vast seas that lay beyond the cliffs. Beriadan had told me that the lord of the ocean would be the best person to ask about my origin. I had to figure out a way to get a hold of him before we left. I had to know.

"Miriam?" I shook myself and half-turned to find Xander a few feet behind me. His expression was one of concern. "Is something the mater?"

I smiled and walked up to him to loop my arm through one of his. "Yeah. I was just thinking how I was going to stay awake until midnight."

He chuckled as he led me down the stairs. "A good meal of fish and a short nap, and I am sure you will be as you have always been: lively and beautiful."

My eyes flickered to our right and the soft waters of the bay. My gut feeling was telling me trouble was coming, and change. Lots of it.

CHAPTER 4

We returned to the house for a feast of fish. I napped until the appointed hour when I was roused from my slumber by a gentle but firm hand on my shoulder.

I buried my face in the pillows of the bed. "Go away. The sun's not up."

Xander's soft chuckle floated over me. "The sun is several hours away, but our meeting with Dreail is very soon."

I creaked open an eye and glared at him. He looked perfectly awake and handsome in the light of the candle he held in one hand. "How do you do it?"

He tilted his head to one side. "How do I do what?"

I sat up and rubbed my bleary eyes. "How can you be so gorgeous all the time?"

Xander smiled and offered me his hand. "I find that being among among friends and the woman I love have a profoundly positive effect on my physical features."

I snorted and took his hand, and he pulled me up. "Flattery will get you-" My mouth opened wide in a yawn.

"Would you like me to carry you down to the beach?" he offered.

I glared at him. "I'm sleepy, not paralyzed, now let's go get spooked."

I took his hand and dragged him out of our bedroom on the second floor. We had a great view of the beach from the windows, a beach that was at that time alight with a large bonfire captured in the center of a ring of large stones. Large, long logs surrounded the stones, and on one of them our group found Dreail.

He stood as Xander, Spiros, Darda, and I approached. "Good night to you all."

Xander bowed his head as he steered me onto one of the logs. "Good night to you, Dreail. What tales have you brought for our enjoyment?"

Dreail resumed his seat and eyed us with his keen old gaze. "You mentioned you were wanting to hear about banshees, but what kind of tales were you wanting? Something I heard as a lad in the ports of the world? Or maybe something from my own adventures?"

"Perhaps a local tale will be a good start, and one rooted in history," Xander suggested.

Dreail's face fell and his voice grew quiet as he gravely nodded his head. "I know the one you're wanting, My Lord. Don't think ol' Dreail has forgotten it, for that is certainly one from my own life I won't forget till my dying day."

Goosebumps speckled my skin. I scooted closer to Xander. "So it's a true story?"

He gave a nod. "Aye, My Lady. True as all of us sitting around this camp fire." He glanced over his shoulder to the cliff on the left. "And as true as the day I saw her jump. Of course, she was dead already, but I didn't know that."

I yelped when I felt something touch my left arm. Xander chuckled beside me as he finished wrapping his arm around me. "Should we avoid this tale?"

I glared up at him, but cuddled closer. "I'm just cold, that's all." I glanced at Dreail and nodded. "Go ahead. I want to hear it."

He pursed his lips and gazed into the fire. The crackling flames cast long, dancing shadows over his face. "Twas five and a half centuries ago that I first heard the tale of the banshee that haunted the northern cliff. Even then it was an ancient story passed on from my great-grandfather through the line down to me."

My eyes widened. "How old are you?"

He picked up the poker and stabbed at the fire. "I will be celebrating my five-hundred and sixty-first birthday this year, My Lady."

I glanced from him to Xander and pointed a finger at him. "And you're how old again?"

"Over three hundred," he reminded me.

"What is the tale, Captain Dreail?" Darda spoke up.

He tossed another log into the hungry fire and held his hands out. "The bay wasn't always so peaceful. There used to be quite a bit of fishing along these shores before the rich folks come in with their money and built up the houses as they are. Twas the way most people made their living then. The ships with their white sails would go out into the ocean as big as a cloud and come back like plumes of smoke as each caught their catch."

I tilted my head back and watched the plumes of smoke rise from the fire and sail into the dark, star-lit sky. Dreail raised his arm and cut the plume in two, parting them like the water parted the cliffs. "It is a simple life, but dangerous. The seas are unforgiving. They resent a fisherman catching its fish, and bring storms to remind the people to watch their greed." He curled his hand into the smoke. The plume separated into bunches that bumped together like the rocking waves of a stormy sea.

I caught my mouth hanging open and snapped it shut before I glanced at the others. Spiros and Darda were likewise enraptured. Xander met my gaze and smiled before he pressed a finger to his lips and pointed back at our storyteller.

"A young woman, a maiden of the fields, fell in love with one of the men of the sea," he continued as the smoke merged into the plume once again. "They were to be married in the lord's house, the one in which you're staying. Then a storm came. Twas a terrible strong storm that battered the bay and broke apart the docks. The ships sailed in from their fishing with their sails torn to pieces. The young woman stood on the beach with many other folks and looked for the ships. Out of the two dozen that left that early morning, five were missing. Her lover was aboard one of them." He stretched out both hands and his fingers danced across the smoke. Short white figures formed and appeared to be looking into the bay. "She waited through the long day, and still nothing was heard of the missing ships. Everyone took them for lost and told the young woman to do the same. She wouldn't hear none of it and rushed onto the northern cliff."

His hands moved faster through the smoke. A small cloud ran through the dark sky above the plume. "The winds were at their strongest. None dared follow her to the mouth of the bay where she stopped on the edge. Something in the water caught her attention. Twas a body of a young man floating on his back."

"Her lover?" I guessed.

He nodded. "Aye, her betrothed. His empty eyes stared up at her. The sight drove her mad. She leapt into the stormy sea and fell onto his body, dragging them both to the watery depths." He flung his arms downward and eradicated the picture. The smoke floated into the sky and disappeared out of view. He dropped his arms into his lap and shook his head. "That was the last anyone saw of their bodies. The tide never brought them home."

"Only their bodies?" Spiros spoke up.

Dreail nodded. "Aye, for the spirit of the unhappy woman returned as a banshee. Her cursed soul walks the northern cliff during the worst of storms, and at the worst of it she makes her terrible cry before she plunges into the sea."

I shivered. "How awful to have to go through that again and again."

He set his steady eyes on me. "Aye, tis not a fate I would wish on anyone, especially after I saw it for myself. Twas a stormy morning that I took out the boat by myself, my father being sick with a fever and stuck in bed. My mother warned me not to go out. The banshee would come. I scoffed at her words. The tale was an old fable told to frighten children from the coast on stormy days." He looked at the fire and shook his head. "If only I'd listened to her."

"But you returned without harm," Darda pointed out.

OCEANS BENEATH DRAGONS

He lifted his head and frowned at her. "Not all harm is done to the body, My Lady. The mind can be just as scarred, and maybe worse."

"They say telling your troubles is good for the soul," Xander spoke up.

Dreail nodded. "Aye, it does no harm, and perhaps it saves another from my own stupid mistake. I took my father's ship out. No one else sailed that day but me. The bay was a choppy mess of waves that rocked the boat something fierce. I couldn't unfurl the sail more than halfway without fear it would be torn apart. I reached the opening between the cliffs when I heard it. That horrible sound of agony."

"Like the alarm from the barracks?" I guessed.

He met my eyes and shook his head. "No, My Lady. The call of the banshee is far worse. It sinks into you and clings to your soul like fog on a cold day, and there it stays as the wailing beats at your ears, driving you to the brink of madness." He leaned forward and studied the fire with such intensity that I wondered if he would throw himself into it. His soft, low voice broke the heavy silence. "I begged for death that night, My Lady, if only that terrible wailing would stop. Begged for it rather than slip into the madness it threatened me with."

I swallowed the lump in my throat. "What happened?"

He leaned back and stared up at the dark sky as though looking at the tops of the cliffs on that fateful day. "That's when I saw her. She stood up on the cliff all clad in white, her dress clinging to her body and her hair whipping to and fro like a serpent.

The cliff rises fifty feet above the water, but I saw her face as clearly as I see yours. It was terrible to behold. Her eyes were white and glowing, but empty like the treacherous whirlpools to the far north. Her mouth was open in that hideous cry of hers."

"Did you not wish to flee?" Darda spoke up.

He shook his head. "I was caught, My Lady, caught in the grip of that terrible sound. It tried to pull me apart, but not like the giant mathair shuigh. This tore me apart from the inside. I cowered in the bottom of that boat praying for anything to end it, or me, and that's when she raised her arms-" he straightened and stretched out his own arms, "-and with one long, final wail she fell over the other side of the cliff. I heard a splash and nothing more." He dropped his arms into his lap and shook his head. "I was free of her cursed wailing and made for shore. One of my uncles met me at the dock to tell me my father had taken a turn for the worse. I reached his side a few minutes before the gods took him, and have never sailed the bay on a stormy day since."

Our storyteller hung his head and we fell into a heavy silence. I pursed my lips and glanced up at Xander. He stood and caught the attention of all present as he bowed to Dreail. "Please accept my apologies, Captain. I had no idea the story effected you so and would not have asked-" Dreail raised his head and one hand, and shook his head.

"No, My Lord, I won't be having that. I'm glad to be telling my tale to any who wish to hear it. All I ask is that you remember my tales and not go sailing on a stormy sea, for the banshee always takes her due against those who trespass on her sorrow." He rose to his feet and groaned. "But perhaps that's all for this night. You will be staying a spell, My Lord?"

Xander nodded. "Yes, for a few weeks."

Dreail smiled and nodded. "Good. Plenty of time for more stories. I'll bid you all goodnight."

"Goodnight," we softly returned.

The old captain turned away from us and shuffled southward down the beach, a lonely shadow beneath the dark night sky.

CHAPTER 5

We extinguished the fire and returned to the house. I seated myself on the edge of our bed as Xander undressed himself. My mind was too preoccupied by Dreail's stories to admire the view.

"So that really happened to him? His father dying and everything?" I spoke up.

Xander didn't pause in his undressing as he nodded his head. "Yes. He inherited his father's ship and left the bay for many years. I met him on some of his travels. By that time he was well-versed in the geography of much of the world's oceans and assisted me in defeating Magnus's fleet."

"How'd that happen" I asked him.

"We positioned ourselves with the tide so our rowers could be used to man the guns."

OCEANS BENEATH DRAGONS

I scooted back and curled my lips against my chest so I could rest my chin on my knees. "So how old do you think the banshee is?"

Xander finished his dressing and seated himself beside me. "The story is very ancient, perhaps as old as the wars between humans and dragons some seven thousand years ago."

I winced. "That's a long time to be haunting a cliff and ruining other peoples' lives."

His bright green eyes studied me. "She is a woman to be pitied, but do not fret over what cannot be changed. Fate is often cruel, and one false step may be all that is needed for an eternity of regret.

"But that? To be stuck up there on the cliff going through that again and again?" I persisted.

He closed his eyes and shook his head. "I cannot say that the punishment fit her final madness in taking her life, but perhaps some day she will find her peace with her lover." He leaned down and smiled at me. "I am fortunate not to have such an insurmountable obstacle to overcome to be with mine."

I rolled my eyes and pushed him away. "Hold off on that for a bit, Romeo. I want an explanation about dragons and aging, like how come Dreail is only a hundred years older than you but he looks like he could be your grandfather."

Xander sat up straight. "Dragons enjoy the prime of their life for several centuries, aging only a year when decades have passed. The aging process often reverts back to that of a human at around five-hundred years, though perhaps later."

My shoulders slumped. "So I've missed a lot of your best years?"

He wrapped his arms around me and smiled down at me. "These are my best years. Never doubt that."

I leaned my cheek against his chest and closed my eyes. His sweet warmth soaked into me, eliciting a pleasant reaction from my body. "I guess I can believe."

Xander's hands wandered down to my waist where his fingers teased the band of my jeans. "Seeing is believing, my love."

I looked up at him and smiled. "Then make me a believer."

"With pleasure."

He leaned down and captured my lips in a heated kiss. His hands deftly unbuttoned my jeans and slipped them over my hips. The pert peaks of my breasts pressed against his hard chest as I moaned into our kiss. He broke us apart and blazed a hot, wet trail of sensual love down my neck.

I wrapped my arms around his neck and closed my eyes as I reveled in the feel of his hard body against my soft, pliable one. "How can you be this good?"

He lifted his head and slyly smiled at me. "I can be better with more practice."

I opened my eyes and grinned at him. "Then practice away."

"Gladly."

He pressed our lips together in a hot, passionate kiss as he lay me across the bed with him over me. His hands massaged my smooth hips before one of them slipped up and pressed against my wet underwear. I broke us apart and gasped as he stroked me with his fingers. My hips rocked in time with his sensual motion. I clutched his shoulders and groaned.

His other hand slid my underwear over my hips and he slipped a finger between my warm, wet walls. I leaned my head back and moaned as he teased my sensitive flesh. Every motion was sweet, delicious torture. I wanted the pleasure to last forever, but the tension was unbearable. I needed release. I needed *him*.

"Please," I moaned.

He leaned forward and brushed his lips against my ear. "Please what?"

His finger stroked me nice and hard. I shuddered. "Please take me."

His wicked chuckle vibrated through me. "Not yet, my Maiden. Just a little more."

He pulled my shirt and bra over my head and revealed my pert, swollen breasts. They glistened with sweat and heaved up and down in time with my quick, shallow breaths.

I was now completely naked beneath his prying, lust-filled eyes. I arched my back and reveled in the feel of my naked flesh atop the smooth covers. The bulge in his pants revealed his strong need for me. He leaned down and nipped at my small, tight buds. His finger never stopped pleasuring me. He stroked harder and longer. My hips moved faster and faster. The tension inside of me built higher and deeper, but I was still not satisfied. I was empty. I needed him to fill me.

I groaned and squirmed. My voice was deep and hoarse. "Oh god, Xander. Please take me."

He grunted and drew away long enough to tear his clothes off himself. He draped his body over mine and pressed his thick, stiff manhood deep into my wet core. I wrapped my arms around his neck and sighed in relief.

His thrusts started as long and gentle. I could feel the tension in his tight muscles. His teeth were clenched. I brushed away some of his hair from his face and smiled up at him. "Don't hold back."

My gentle command was gladly received. He wrapped his arms around me and thrust harder. His penetrations were now fast and deep. Every stroke pressed against my bundle of nerves and sent shots of tingling pleasure through me. I closed my eyes and sank into the depths of frenzied lust as he took me with each hard, deep thrust.

My groans slipped into quick gasps, and those changed into loud, clear calls of encouragement. "Yes! Yes! Oh god, yes!"

He grunted and pushed faster. I couldn't keep up. My body tightened. I felt the sweeping waves of orgasm lap at my muscles.

My blissful end came in a brilliant flash of light. I arched my back and cried out my glee for all the world to know. He continued to push into me, stretching my pleasure nearly beyond my limits.

Xander tensed above me. His teeth were clenched. The green of his brilliant eyes glowed in the darkness of the night.

Then it was finished. He fell beside me. My body slumped down atop the sheets. I wiggled and groaned. "That's gonna hurt tomorrow." Xander chuckled. I looked to my right and saw one of his green eyes laughing at me. I frowned. "What?"

He raised himself onto his arms and smiled down at me. "I would not have performed well if you did not feel some discomfort the day after."

OCEANS BENEATH DRAGONS

I snorted. "No matter what world all the guys are the same."

Xander lay on his side and wrapped his arms around me to pull me against his warm body. "I hope I am not the same as others you have met."

I snuggled against his chest and closed my eyes as I smiled. "Only if the guys in my world hid their wings really well." A thought hit me. I glanced up at my lover. "So when did dragons disappear from my world, anyway?"

He closed his eyes and shook his head. "I cannot tell. All my ancestors know is the last communication was many thousands of years ago."

I leaned my head against him and furrowed my brow. "It's weird that they died out. I mean, you guys are a lot more powerful than humans."

"Fate is an unpredictable arbiter of life," he mused.

I closed my eyes and sighed. "You're telling me."

Sleep slipped over me, and I dreamed of flying men among skyscrapers.

CHAPTER 6

I awoke to the gentle sound of waves against soft sand. Sunlight streamed into our bedroom as I lay on my side. I stretched and opened my eyes.

The flat spot beside me was empty. The covers showed obvious signs of use, but the person who used them was gone. I touched the sheets. Slightly warm. He must have left within the last half hour.

I sat up and rubbed one eye as I looked over our spacious chamber. The dresser, bed and a small table were all carved from gray driftwood, giving the room an aged appearance. The walls were an aged oak from the forests that surrounded the serene valley. I breathed in deep and leapt from the bed. My wrinkled clothes from previous evening were still on me. I was ready to hunt for my dragon lord.

I slipped out of the bedroom and down the hall to the foyer. My feet barely made a sound. Nothing else in the house did. I reached the front door and grasped the handle.

"Xander is in the other direction." I yelped and spun around to find Spiros standing not more than two feet behind me. He had a mischievous smile on his face as he bowed his head to me. "Good morning, My Lady."

I clutched my chest over my heart and glared at him. "Are you trying a royal assassination through scaring me to death?"

He raised his eyes to me and shook his head. "I would never dream of frightening you, My Lady."

I dropped my hand and eyed him with suspicion. "Uh-uh. You said Xander was somewhere?"

He stepped aside and gestured to the hall that led to the patio. "He is on the beach to the south of the house. Would you care for me to lead you?"

I snorted. "No. You might finish the job. I'll go find him."

I strode past the mischievous captain and down the hall to the patio. The area was empty, but I walked to the railing and leaned out for a view of the beach some eight feet below me. To my right and some fifty feet off sat Xander. He was perched at the bottom of the slope and atop one of the few large rocks that were found scattered over the length of the beach. I climbed down the stone steps to the sand and crunched over to him.

I expected to find the dragon lord in some pensive reverie as he looked out over the sand to the water that gently lapped against the beach. Instead, his head was tilted down so he stared at his hands that were upright in his lap. My foot kicked a pebble and sent it clattering across its brethren. He looked up from his work and smiled even as he hid one hand on his other side.

"You have risen early," he commented as I plopped down beside him.

"I thought I'd start a new habit," I returned as I leaned forward to look at his other side. He drew his hand back into my view. It was empty.

He chuckled. "You are a horrible liar."

I nodded at his side. "What do you got there?"

Xander shook his head. "Nothing of importance."

I snorted. "You're a horrible liar, and you shouldn't keep secrets from your Maiden."

He chuckled. "This would be the most appropriate place to do so."

I raised an eyebrow. "Why?"

He nodded at the waters. "In the ancient tongue of Cayden's people this bay is called Bha na Ruin."

"And the means what?" I asked him.

"It means 'Bay of Secrets.'"

I leaned back and grinned. "Nice name, but I think you're just trying to distract me from what you're hiding in your pocket."

He bowed his head. "I will accept your comment without argument, but I am glad you have come." He stood and wiped the sand off him before he stretched out his hand to me. "I was about to inquire about our dinner when you arrived. Care to join me?"

I furrowed my brow, but took his hand. "I'd rather walk along the beach."

Xander smiled and drew me against him as we set off in the opposite direction of the house and toward the southern cliff. "That is exactly what I intend us to do."

I jerked my head over my shoulder. "Shouldn't we be heading that way for the kitchen?"

He shook his head. "No. On this trip our kitchen is the vast expanse of water."

I glanced past him at the calm, glistening bay water. "I hope you're not implying that everyone is going to rely on me for their dinner because we might have a starvation mutiny on our hands."

Xander nodded at small sailing ship that navigated through the cliffs and broke the calm bay waters. It drew up beside a dock to which Xander led me. "I believe that until we have fully tested your skills we will rely on a more seasoned provider."

Dreail hopped from the ship onto the dock with a thick rope in one hand. He bent down beside a thick post and tied up the rope faster than I tied my shoelaces.

I looked up at Xander as we walked down the noisy planks. "Is he already done fishing?"

"Yes. He leaves in the early morning hours and returns shortly after the sunrise."

Dreail glanced up and squinted at us. His face brightened when he saw our faces, and he stood and gave a slight nod. "Good morning to you, My Lord. What can I do for you?"

"We wish to purchase some fish from you, provided the catch was good," Xander told him.

Dreail nodded. "As good a catch as any." He stepped into the ship and lifted the lid of a wood box. Inside flopped dozens of fish of various sizes. "You can pick out whatever you like from it."

Xander looked to me and gestured to the box of wriggling life. "Care to do the honors?"

I held up one hand and shook my head. "No thanks. I prefer to pick out my food from a plate."

He chuckled and stepped onto the ship. I glanced down the dock at the parting of the cliffs. My mind wandered back to Beriadan's advice: *If you wish to know yourself, seek out Valtameri. He will know your lineage.*

I walked down the planks to the end of the dock. A ladder some five feet on the right side of the dock led down into the water. The depth was so great that I couldn't see the bottom. There was only darkness. That darkness held answers. All I had to do was be brave enough and catch the attention of the big fish of the sea.

A strong gust blew over me. I closed my eyes, took a deep breath, and stepped off the dock.

That deep breath was probably what saved my life. I plunged feet-first into the cool water of the bay. My head was submerged, but my natural buoyancy brought me back to the surface. Pity nothing else of me wanted to cooperate. I still didn't know how to swim. My arms flailed about me and my legs kicked together. The result was I was sinking, and fast.

I reached for the dock, but the waves drew me away and toward the far shore. The water splashed over me and I swallowed a filling dose. "Help!"

Xander glanced over his shoulder. A coy smile slipped onto his face as he stepped onto the dock and knelt at the edge close by where I floundered. "It appears we are both keeping secrets. Have you taught yourself to swim without my knowing?"

I took in another gulp of water that made me sputter. "No!"

Xander's eyes widened a half second before he swan-dove into the water. He barely left a wake which was good because I couldn't handle the tiniest of splashes. My head went under and the weight of my wet clothes made sure I stayed under. I watched Xander swim to me as swift as a fish. He wrapped his arm around me and kicked. We broke the surface and I gasped for air.

Xander drew us over to the ladder and pushed me against the rungs. Dreail was there to help me up the thin strips of wood and onto the dock. I collapsed atop the boards and Xander soon knelt beside me. A coughing fit overtook me. I stretched my neck out and spit up cup of water.

Xander rubbed my back. "Are you injured at all?"

I managed to get my fit mostly under control and glanced over my shoulder at him. "You're-*cough*-asking that a lot-*cough*-on this trip."

He smiled. "It is only because I care."

"Your Lady has taken a lot of water," Dreail commented.

"I'll be fine," I choked out as I sat up. I managed a weak, shaky smile at the pair of men. "Just give me a towel and a nice spot in the sun and I'll be fine."

"I will escort you back to the house," Xander offered as he helped me to my feet. He glanced at Dreail. "If you would oblige me by waiting, I will return for the fish."

Dreail bowed his head. "No harm waiting a while, My Lord. I will be hauling them to my house and you can choose them there."

"Then we will see you within the hour," Xander promised.

My dragon lord swept me into his arms and carried me across the dock toward land. I glared at him. "I'm wet, not paralyzed. Let me walk."

"Your legs are unsteady, and I would rather you were set down on land," he argued.

I glared, but movement behind us caught my attention. I glanced over his shoulder at the solitary fisherman. "Does Dreail have any family?"

Xander looked ahead as he shook his head. "None that I know of, though I have heard that in his youth he dallied a great deal with human and dragon women."

I grinned. "So he could have some children somewhere?"

"It is possible."

I leaned forward close to Xander's face and studied him. "You don't happen to have any dragon children flying around somewhere, do you?"

He smiled and his mischievous eyes flickered to me. "Do you wish to meet them?"

I crossed my arms over my chest and frowned. "That better be a joke."

He chuckled. "Very much so. While I have dallied, I have not sired anyone, at least not to my knowledge." His eyes flickered down to me and his smile took a lecherous turn. "Though I am eager to sire a child."

I spread my arms and let the water drip off them. "Let's wait until I'm not covered in seawater."

CHAPTER 7

We reached the house and Xander carried me onto the patio. A wood bench stood against the northern wall. He set me down with my legs hanging over and took a seat beside me.

I leaned my back against the stone wall that acted as a railing and ran a hand through my wet hair. My fingers got tangled in the mess. I snorted. "You'd think if I'm going to kill myself I'd not make such a mess of it and myself." I yanked on the knots in my hair, but the hair wouldn't unbind.

Xander grabbed my hand and pulled it away before he scooted up to my back. His deft fingers worked away at the tangles, and I felt the strands fall free from one another.

I closed my eyes and enjoyed his soft touch. "You're really good at this."

He chuckled. "As a child I was fond of watching my mother brush her hair. It was one of the few times during the day when we were left to ourselves. She would often allow me to brush her hair as I regaled her with my day of training."

"Whittling training?" I teased him.

He shook his head. "No. The less agreeable schooling and military training."

I opened my eyes and turned my head to stare at him with one eye. "But I thought you liked fighting. You're really good at it."

Xander finished his pulling and took a seat beside me. He gazed out on the calm waters and furrowed his brow. "One is not always good at what they wish to be, and not always terrible at what they dislike."

I leaned forward to catch his eye. "So you're good at what you don't like and good at what you like?"

He looked to me and smiled. "I am not as good at protecting you as I would wish."

I snorted and looked ahead. "I'm not exactly helping with all these suicide attempts."

Xander studied my face and frowned. "Why did you wish to drowned yourself?".

I shrugged. "I thought it'd be fun." The stern look from him killed the humor. My shoulders sagged and I turned my face away. "I thought I could get someone's attention."

He furrowed his brow. "You already have my complete attention. Is that not-" I shook my head.

"Not yours." I raised my head and nodded at the deep water. "The fae that lives down there. The big boy of the sea."

Xander arched his eyebrow. "You wished to make contact with Valtameri?"

I shrank and my eyes flickered to him. "Was that a bad idea?"

"You shouldn't tempt gods to help you in a spot you've put yourself in, Your Ladyship," the old sea dog spoke up.

Xander nodded. "He is correct. While the Mare Fae, and Valtameri in particular, are considered gods by many, they are not omnipotent. It was not a wise choice to test his attentiveness by throwing yourself into the bay."

I drew my legs against my chest and set my chin on one knee. "I just wanted to learn who or what I was. How I'm able to do some of the things I do with all that glowing light in my hands." I sighed and shrugged. "And if that didn't work out then maybe I'd learn how to swim. Everybody else makes it look so easy I thought I'd be a cinch."

Xander stretched his arm across my shoulders and drew me against his warm chest. The bright sun and my damp clothes made me a little lightheaded as I listened to the beat of the dragon's heart. His soft voice sounded far away as he stroked my untangled hair. "Does it bother you not knowing why you are able to perform miracles?"

I tilted my head back and looked up into his pensive expression. "Wouldn't it bother you?"

He shook his head. "No, at least not enough to risk my life. What is most important is what you do with your skills, not how they came to be."

I sank against him and pursed my lips. "I'd still like to know. . ."

"Perhaps fate will grant you your answers soon, but for the present we shall work on your swimming," he suggested.

A commotion out front caught our attention. Xander stood and leaned out over the railing for a look. A smile slipped onto his lips and he glanced over his shoulder at me. "It appears that Cayden and his Maiden have arrived even earlier than I anticipated."

I turned around and leaned on the wide stone railing. "Stephanie's with him?"

The commotion moved from the front into the house and down the hall. In a moment Cayden strode onto the patio and behind him came Stephanie with Spiros close behind them.

Stephanie's face lit up when she saw me and she rushed over to give me a good hug. "Oh, how glad I am to see you!"

I pulled us apart and studied her. She was tanned and wore a becoming white summer dress with a wide-brimmed straw hat. I smiled. "You look like a regular lady and here I am in my old clothes." I glanced down at my human-world clothes that I still wore.

She took a seat beside me and shook her head. "You look wonderful in them, but you're soaked. What happened?"

"I went for a swim without my swimming suit," I told her.

The men greeted each other less joyously. Xander grasped Cayden's hand in both of his and smiled at him. "I am pleased you could join us so soon. Have the raiders been subdued or do they still steal pork chops in the middle of the night?"

Cayden pursed his lips and shook his head. "I fear this is no laughing matter, Lord Xander. We have arrived early because the raiders were sighted along this part of the coast."

OCEANS BENEATH DRAGONS

Xander's good humor fell from his face and his eyebrows crashed down. "They have not been checked? Surely human raiders are no match for your defenses. What have they that stops your men from burning their ships with their fire?"

A dark shadow settled on the young dragon lord's face. "They have learned not only how to extinguish our flame, but to relinquish us of our wings and scales."

My dragon lord arched an eyebrow. "How?"

Cayden closed his eyes and shook his head. "We cannot fathom what magic they use, but whenever the coastal defenders have met them in battle over their ships the humans launch sticky balls from catapults positioned on their decks. Even the slightest touch of the ball reverts a dragon to their human form and they tumble into the waters. It is all my men can do to rescue their own and not be hit themselves, much less defend against the raiders. Many refuse to fight when they see that their companions cannot even spread their wings for a fortnight, leaving the coast woefully undefended." He turned his face away. "My men are brave, but this magic is too much for their courage. They have taken to calling this dreadful weapon Dragon Bane."

Xander set his hand on Cayden's shoulder. "No one who knows your men could doubt their courage, my friend, and against such odds a retreat and new strategy would not be considered cowardly. What remedies have been tried on those afflicted by this magic?"

Cayden pursed his lips and stared hard at the ground. "Everything. The doctors are at their wits end. They have no more herbs and waters to try to lift the curse. The magicians have tried their hands, but they say there is no magic present with which to combat."

Xander dropped his hand and furrowed his brow. "That points to a natural source for their weapon, but I cannot think of what herbs could create such a concoction. Do you know if it has any effect on humans?"

Cayden shook his head. "There is no effect at all. Several of our human allies ingested the balls, and nothing happened to them."

"Very perplexing. . ." Xander mused.

"What about Dreail?" I spoke up.

Cayden raised an eyebrow. "Captain Dreail? What does he know of these troubles?"

I shrugged before I looked to Xander. "He might know something. You said he traveled a lot when he was younger. Maybe he knows how to beat these balls, or at least maybe he's heard about it."

Xander nodded. "Your idea has merit. Captain Dreail knows of many legends. He may know of this one. We shall see him at once."

CHAPTER 8

Our small group, two Maidens and three dragon warriors, walked along the beach road to an old stone house close to the start of the southern cliffs. Dreail sat outside on an overturned barrel and stared down at his hands. One hand held a piece of wood while the other gripped a knife. His knife-hand moved swiftly across the wood and whittled the piece into a long, round shape.

He looked up at our coming and stood before he inclined his head. "An honor it is to have the company of two lords here at my old home."

Cayden and Xander both bowed their heads. "The honor is ours," Xander replied as he glanced down at Dreail's hand that held the wood. "A lure?"

Dreail grinned and nodded. "Aye. A big fish stole one of my best ones, and I'll be damned if I'll work without another."

Cayden stepped forward. "Captain Dreail, we have come on most urgent business, and hope your wisdom will be able to help."

The old sea dog arched an eyebrow and pocketed the wood. "Anything I can do to help, My Lord."

"You have no doubt heard of the troubles along the southern coast?" Cayden asked him.

Dreail nodded. "Aye. A bit messy with those human raiders. Have they come here?"

Cayden shook his head. "No, but they approach, and with them they bring a new weapon, one which we cannot stop. It afflicts our soldiers so they lose all of their dragon attributes for a fortnight. We hoped you might know of this weapon, and how we might combat it."

Dreail rubbed his chin with one leathered hand. "You say that dragons are stuck in their human forms?"

The young dragon lord nodded. "Yes. They are struck by a sticky ball that renders them as humans for a fortnight."

Dreail dropped his hand and frowned. "Do you know where these raiders come from?"

"They are the inhabitants of the islands of Ui Breasail," Cayden told him.

The old captain nodded. "As I suspected. That is your problem there, My Lord."

Cayden blinked at him and shook his head. "I fail to see the connection, captain."

Dreail resumed his seat on the overturned barrel and nodded his head. "Aye, and that's no fault of your own, My Lord. The tale I have was passed on from one of their own maidens many a year ago. She was my sweetheart for a time some fifty years ago and I expect she wanted me to marry her, but I was still restless then. Maybe that is why she parted in me an old tale passed down through her family. It was a tale of the founding of the humans on the island, and how they fought the dragons who sought to take it from them."

"But there has never been a struggle between the humans of Ui Breasail and our people," Cayden argued.

Dreail scoffed. "A land like Ui Breasail deserves to be fought over. The land is blessed by a spring of water that flows from their highest mountain and provides fresh water to the fields and people. The forests grow aplenty with trees and fruits so that one needn't look far for food. They grow an abundance of sheep there, or they did when I last visited, and ship the wool off to the north where they are in greater need of the warmth than these sunny shores."

"But what of these humans on Ui Breasail?" Spiros asked him.

"My lady friend told me how her ancestors fought off the dragons with some herbs that only grew on those islands. She said it would make them forget their dragon selves for a while," he told us.

Xander glanced at Cayden. "That does hint at your current troubles."

Cayden nodded. "Yes, it does. Did all the humans know of this tale?"

Dreail shook his head. "None but my lady friend. Twas her family who prepared the herbs, and she was all a-bragging about how the recipe was kept in the family." He snorted. "She was the last of them, too, or so she said, and wanted the line to continue. I got the hint and set sail soon after that."

"Do you recall her family name?" Xander spoke up.

Dreail furrowed his brow. "It was something like Mac Bradaigh. I remember because she was as spirited as her family name." He smile and shook his head. "A fine lass, she was. I expect she went to the gods long ago."

Xander's eyes flickered to Cayden. "We shall see, will we not?"

Cayden pursed his lip and nodded. "Yes. I can see no other way than to meet with the humans and learn why they have attacked us. If diplomacy fails, we shall have to resort to stealing away those who created this weapon."

"And if that fails?" I spoke up. Cayden averted his eyes from mine. I frowned. "What if you can't get this family off the island? What then?"

Xander set a hand on my shoulder. "We shall hope and try for the best outcome, and plan for the worst possibility."

Dreail looked to Cayden. "My Lord, I know I ask much of you when I say that I would like her family to be brought here where I might see them."

Cayden smiled and shook his head. "You do not ask for too much, captain. Without your help we would not be as well-informed as we are now."

The old sea dog smiled and inclined his head. "I am much obliged to you, My Lord, and good journey to you."

"A journey that shall have to wait a day," Cayden commented as he turned to Xander. "We must charter a ship to take us over there, and since I will not risk any fishing vessels we shall have to wait a day for the fleet to arrive at the base just to the south of here."

Xander looked to me with a soft smile. "A day is short when spent in fine company, and I believe I promised you a swimming lesson."

OCEANS BENEATH DRAGONS

"If you're looking for a good teacher you can't go wrong with Lady Abha," the fisherman spoke up.

Xander looked to him and arched an eyebrow. "Does she still reside here?"

He nodded. "Aye, at the house against the northern cliffs. Says it gives her the chance to swim in the open ocean and the bay, if she's of mind."

Xander bowed his head to Dreail. "We are in your debt for your valuable information."

Dreail wrinkled his nose and waved his hand. "Never you mind that. Just be careful when you journey to the Ui Breasail. The humans there are a fierce people, but they're proud, too. If you make too many demands they'll be throwing you off the island, or worse."

"We will heed your warning and be mindful of our demands," Cayden assured him.

Dreail slid off the barrel. "Good. Now I'm sure you'll be wanting your fish."

We exchanged our goodbyes and left with a basket full of large, fat fish. Cayden and Xander walked together with Spiros behind them while Stephanie and I made a team behind the soldierly captain.

Cayden leaned toward Xander and lowered his voice so I barely overheard his words. "I wish to speak with Spiros and you alone when we return to the house."

"After breakfast," Xander promised him.

I frowned and opened my mouth to make a smart comment, but my attention was diverted when Stephanie looped her arms through one of mine. She smiled up at me. It was a brighter and more confident smile than I remembered. "Would you mind if I joined your swimming lessons? Cayden's realm is full of lakes, but I don't swim very well so I can't enjoy them as much as I'd like to."

I returned her smile and nodded. "I wouldn't mind, but I don't know about this Lady person." I looked to Xander. "Do you think she'd mind?"

Xander turned his head to one side to glance at us. "That would depend on Lady Abha's temperament when we first find her. She is very firm of mind, and if she promises to teach you both she shall."

"And if she doesn't?" I returned.

He chuckled and stared ahead. "Then the cliffs would crash into the seas before she would teach you."

"You sure there isn't somebody else we can ask?" I inquired.

"She would be the most appropriate to ask for one of your unique heritage," he returned.

"'Unique heritage?'" Stephanie repeated.

I nodded. "Yeah, turns out I'm some sort of a rare fairy in this world."

Her eyes widened. "Then you are a Mare Fae?"

I leaned away and studied her with a teasing grin. "Somebody's been doing their homework."

She smiled and gave a nod. "I wanted to learn as much as I could about our-this world."

I squeezed her arms and stared ahead. "You can call it our world. It's weird, but at least it smells better."

CHAPTER 9

We reached the house and went in for breakfast. A plate of fried fish and a stack of soft, fluffy biscuits waited for us on the small but comfortable dining table. The food was soon consumed and the three dragon men rose from their seats.

I stood as well, but Xander gestured to Stephanie. "Perhaps you would like to show your friend the beach and the docks. We will join you shortly."

I arched an eyebrow. "More secrets?"

My dragon lord smiled. "Merely a matter of business. We would rather not bore you with affairs of state."

Stephanie curled her arms around one of mine and pulled me toward the hall. "I would very much like to see the beach."

I pursed my lips, but allowed her to lead me down the hall to the patio. The men followed us halfway down the passage, but turned into a room on the right.

I stepped onto the patio and sighed. "I still wish I knew what they were talking about. . ."

Stephanie smiled and tugged on my arm. "Cayden wouldn't have let us in the room, but I have another idea. This way."

"What are you-hey!"

She pulled me down the stairs and around to the right side of the house where we stopped. A line of windows sat ten feet above the sand and grass. The wall below the windows was hidden beneath a couple of stacks of barrels and lobster traps.

I looked to Stephanie and grinned. "I like the way you think."

She blushed and turned her face away. "It's nothing, really."

I changed our roles and took her hand to tug her to the base of the mess. One of the piles climbed up to a window of the room our dragon boys were in. I grabbed a barrel and shook it. The whole structure shifted a little. I cringed and looked to Stephanie. "Let's go up one at a time. I'll go first."

Stephanie shrank back and pressed one hand against her stomach. "I'm not so sure about that."

"It's easy. Let me show you." I eased myself on top of the barrel. The mess shook a little, but held together as I climbed the ten feet to the window. The faint sound of voices floated down to me. I peeked my head over the sill and looked inside. Xander, Cayden and Spiros stood together in deep conversation.

OCEANS BENEATH DRAGONS

I glanced down and gestured to her. "Come on! They're already talking!"

Stephanie reluctantly followed me up and together, perched precariously atop the junk, we listened to their conversation.

Cayden pursed his lips. "I am concerned about the consequences of Lord Herod's death, and have received letters from others in the same vein. What shall be done with his lands?"

Xander pursed his lips. "Unfortunately, that is no easy answer to give to you for I have no answer for myself."

"Can they not be divided among us as was done after the Red Dragon's betrayal?" Cayden wondered.

Xander shook his head. "This matter will not be so simple to settle. Herod's lands are larger and not as well-positioned to disperse among the remaining dragon lords. We may be better rewarded if we allowed the people to choose their new lord."

"But if the people chose unwisely?" Spiros argued.

"We cannot help their choice, we can only contain any trouble if it were to arise," Xander countered. He cupped his chin in one hand and furrowed his brow. "What concerns me more is who plotted his demise, and for what purpose."

The young dragon lord started back. "Was it not the human servant who orchestrated the assassination?"

Xander dropped his hand and shook his head. "No, at least not entirely. Herod's Maiden mentioned another whom she referred to as 'Crimson.'" His eyes flickered between them. "The name eludes to our enemy, but how they can have such influence so far from their island of exile I do not know."

Cayden pursed his lips and nodded. "Yes. The Bestia Draconis are not content to raid the other islands. The honor-less cowards have no fear of attacking the northwestern realm when its lord is at a Choosing, nor even the Portal in their old lands." He turned his full attention to Xander. "Did you ever learn how they attacked your southern holdings so quickly and without warning?"

"No, nor can my men find where they went after they destroyed the villages," Xander added.

Cayden frowned and stared hard at the floor. "I wonder if my own realm is now being harassed by them. Perhaps they are the true instigators behind these attacks, and the humans are only their pawns."

Xander slowly nodded his head. "There may be some truth in what you say. We shall know when we travel across the straight to the islands."

"What of the Maidens?" Spiros spoke up.

"They will remain here," Xander insisted. "The threat of war looms and we do not know what danger awaits us on the islands. With our ability to protect them in our dragon forms at risk, the danger is even greater."

Spiros gestured to our window. "They will not be pleased to hear that."

Stephanie and I ducked down and glanced at each other. Her pale face reflected my own. Our sudden movements added to our troubles when the pile on which we stood shuddered.

"Jump!" I yelped.

Stephanie and I pushed off the house and leapt as far as we could away from the stack. The heap collapsed beneath our jump and crashed into a pile of rubble that littered the sand with nets and broken bits of wood. Stephanie and I landed on our feet, but fell onto our sides. We flipped onto our backs and watched a crate bounce down the rubble and onto the sand.

A couple of shadows fell over us. We looked up and winced. Spiros, Cayden and Xander stood over us. Two were not happy, and the captain was bemused.

I grinned and waved at them. "Um, hi. You guys done talking already?"

Xander stooped and held out his hand to me. "Until we can be sure there are not more in the conversation than we know."

I winced, but took his hand and let him pull me to my feet. "We just didn't want to be left out, okay? If we're your Maidens then we've got a stake in making sure these realms are safe, too."

Cayden did the same for Stephanie and she nodded. "She's right. We care about these lands, too, and we just want to help."

Xander caught my gaze and frowned. "We will speak of this later. For the present, I would rather we all enjoy ourselves while the peace lasts."

I crossed my arms, but nodded. "Fine. We'll drop it- for now."

He half-turned away from me and offered me his arm. "Do you still wish to learn how to swim."

I grinned and looped my arm through his. "I'll need it on that island vacation you promised me."

A sly smile slipped onto his lips as he led me down to the beach. The others followed close behind. "You have very crafty ways, my Maiden."

I shrugged. "I try. And speaking of crafty, who's this Lady person, anyway? How do you know her?"

Xander turned us left and we strode down the long beach toward the northern cliffs. "Lady Abha is of a royal bloodline, but not a direct descendant of the current ruling house. As such, she has a great deal of time to spend teaching others what she has gathered from the royal library of her people."

I arched an eyebrow. "She's not another dragon lord, is she?"

He chuckled. "I shall leave that for you to decide. As for how I became acquainted with her, she is the one who taught me to swim."

I snorted. "She must be pretty old by now. You sure she can teach us anything other than the dead man's float?"

He blinked at me. "I am not familiar with that swimming maneuver."

"It's where you float face-down in the water. Like this." I leaned forward to mimic the posture. "You don't kick or move your hands or anything. You just let the current take you."

Both his eyebrows shot up. "I see. You refer to the corpse float."

My face fell. "That name's a little more morbid, but they're probably the same."

He smiled. "She knows a great many more strokes than the corpse float, and while she is many centuries old her appearance is that of a woman hardly out of her prime. Indeed, I would say she is far from fragile."

"Though perhaps not senile," Spiros spoke up.

I glanced over my shoulder at him. "So you know her, too?"

He nodded. "Yes. As Xander was taught to swim so was I. We often made it a point to impress our lovely teacher with races where, I am afraid, the lord always came in last."

Xander straightened and glanced at his captain. "I do not recall having ever lost against you in any swimming races."

Spiros shook his head. "That is not true, My Lord. Surely you recall yourself floundering in my wake."

"I do not. It was you who finished last."

"It was you, My Lord."

By this time we'd reached near the end of the beach. A single, simple stone dwelling rose up before us. The house was a single floor structure with cozy cottage windows and shutters. Its beach wall also had a stone patio, but with a ramp access instead of stairs. Smooth markings in the sand surrounded the house.

I stopped in my tracks and held up my hands. "You know what, how about we decide this here and now?" I pointed a finger at the gentle bay. "You two can go out there and race however far you want, and the guy who survives wins."

Xander and Spiros glanced at each other. Sly smiles slid onto their lips. They broke away from us and strode side-by-side to the shores. We other three followed behind and stopped when they paused fifteen feet away from the water and stripped off their shirts and shoes.

"Are you sure this is wise?" Cayden wondered.

"Honor is at stake, Cayden, and honor must be set right," Xander insisted as he set his folded clothes on the sand.

Spiros did the same and together they faced the calm waters. Xander glanced at his old friend. "To the cliffs?"

Spiros smiled and nodded. "To the cliffs."

I looked past them at the waters. If the men swam straight ahead they would reach the cliffs after two hundred feet. One way.

I gulped and glanced at Xander. "Are you guys serious about this?"

Xander looked over his shoulder and nodded. "Very serious. Wait for us." He turned his attention to Spiros. "Ready?"

Spiros nodded. "Yes."

Cayden, Stephanie and I moved to stand beside them. The young dragon lord stepped forward. "If you two wish to go through with this contest, allow me to start you."

"We would be honored honored," Xander agreed.

Cayden picked up a stick and dragged the tip across the sand in front of the two dragon men. "To the mark." Xander and Spiros stepped up to the line. "Ready yourselves." The pair of contestants dug their toes into the sand. "Start!"

Xander and Spiros rushed forward at the same time and soon hit the water. They waded through the shallows before they dove into the deeper waters. Their arms pumped up and down and allowed their bodies to cut across the bay.

They were a hundred feet out when I noticed something in the calm waters to their left between the swimmers and the cliffs. It looked like a scaly tube that slithered in an arc out of the water. The tube ended in a sharp-pointed tail that disappeared beneath the waves.

OCEANS BENEATH DRAGONS

I whipped my head to Cayden and Stephanie. Their focus lay on the swimmers. I rushed to the edge of the water and cupped my hands around my mouth. "Xander! Spiros! Look beside you!"

My voice didn't carry over the distance as the men continued their pursuit of glory. They swam ten more feet before I saw Spiros yanked beneath the surface. Xander stopped and turned around. Something grabbed him, as well, and pulled him beneath the waters.

CHAPTER 10

Cayden and Stephanie rushed to my sides and we all looked agape at the calm, empty bay. My heart quickened. I cupped my hands to my mouth again. "Xander! Xander!"

Nothing. The water was as calm as the grave. I ran forward and reached the shallow waters before Cayden wrapped his arms around my waist and picked me up.

"You cannot go, Miriam!" he insisted as he turned us around and walked back to the shore.

I twisted around to look over my shoulder. My scream echoed over the waters. "Xander!"

That's when I saw it. A head lifted from the waters, but it wasn't either of the dragons. This was the head of a woman of forty. Her face was narrow and her skin was as pale as cream. The sides of her face were spotted with small dark blotches. She wore a heavy veil that, despite the water, billowed out on either side of her head, but her black shirt clung to her bosom.

The strange woman seemed to float toward us as she didn't use her arms to swim nor could I see her feet behind her. As she reached the shallower waters more of her was revealed. Her lower half was lacking in both clothes and the legs to wear them. From the waist down her body was that of a snake. The cream color of her skin extended to the soft flesh of her snake half. The veil that surrounded her face was actually a snake hood, and the blotches were markings.

Stephanie pointed at the creature. "Cayden!"

Cayden set me down and half-turned to look out on our visitor. He smiled. "There is no need to worry."

I whipped my head to him. "But what Xander and-" My question was answered before it was finished when both competitors appeared out of the water. They were wrapped in the ten feet of snake body that belonged to the women. Both men looked frustrated, but not dead.

I rushed forward and met them at the edge of the water. The snake woman stopped a yard away from me and pulled her snake half toward me. Xander and Spiros were deposited on their feet in front of me. The woman drew her tail back and freed them.

I hurried into the water and wrapped my arms around Xander. "I thought you were dead."

He draped his wet arms around me and drew me closer against him. "There was no need to worry."

I pulled myself away from him and glared up into his face. "No need to worry? You guys suddenly disappear, this creepy snake woman appears, and I'm not supposed to be worried?"

He looked to the serpent woman and smiled. "Miriam Cait, allow me to introduce you to Lady Abha."

I whipped my head to the strange woman and blinked at her. "She-but-what? Why would she want to drown you guys?"

The snake woman slithered closer to us and smiled. Her teeth were a little sharper than normal. "I must apologize. My intention was not for you to be afraid."

I shrank away from the woman. Her fingers ended in sharp talons like those of a dragon, and her eyes were mere slits of yellow. Xander chuckled. "I fear my Maiden is not accustomed to the naga way of scolding a pupil."

She frowned and wagged her finger at him. "You were horrible in your swimming. Your forms all were wrong, so for you I had a lesson to teach."

I tilted my head to one side and blinked at her. "You. . .you were just scolding them?"

She nodded. "Yes. They were no good at their swimming, and I showed them. Their poor forms is why down they went."

"Did you have to keep them down for so long?" I questioned her.

"We dragons have a great lung capacity, though not as great as our more water-proficient cousins," Xander told me.

I glanced up at him and arched an eyebrow. "'Cousins?'"

He nodded. "Yes. The naga and dragons were once the same, but many thousands of years ago we took to the skies and the naga to the oceans."

I pointed at Lady Abha. "So dragons looked like that, or vice versa?"

"Our mutual ancestors were somewhere in-between," he explained.

Lady Abha swept her eyes over our group. "Many of you I am seeing. Some lessons are why you have come?"

Xander nodded. "Yes. Our Maidens wish for some lessons from you, if you would grant them the privilege."

The large snake slithered up to me. She raised one arm and furrowed her brow. "Very weak is this one, but a strength I sense." She dropped my arm and leaned forward so our noses almost touched. Her slitted eyes stared into mine for a few seconds as I tried not to lean backward. "Strange this Maiden of yours. Mare Fae in her I sense, but very weak. You are half, yes?"

I shrugged. "I think so, but I'm not sure."

"Can you hear the Call?" she wondered.

I blinked at her. "The what?"

She leaned away from me and nodded. "Never mind. Teaching you I will be doing. Please be showing me the other Maiden." Stephanie reluctantly stepped forward. Abha slithered in front of her and stretched her upper torso closer to my friend. The snake studied her for a moment before she shook her head and pulled herself back. "This one there will be no teaching."

Stephanie's face fell. Cayden stepped forward with a frown on his face. "Why will you not teach my Maiden, Lady Abha?"

Abha waved her hand. "My refusal is not being an insult, young dragon lord. The lives of your Maiden and your child I will not risk."

Everyone froze. More than one of us had wide eyes. Cayden swallowed the lump in his throat and his voice was a half-octave higher than usual. "I-I do not understand what you mean, Lady Abha."

Abha nodded at Stephanie. "A child is she with. The baby is yours, yes?"

Cayden whipped his head to Stephanie and searched her face. "You. . .you are with child?"

She blushed and turned her face away before she gave a nod. "Yes."

He grasped her hands and slipped in front of her so they faced each other. "Why did you not tell me?"

She stared at the ground and bit her lower lip. "I-I wasn't sure until now. I thought I was just a little late. . ."

Cayden's face lit up with joy. He grasped her waist in his hands and spun her around a few times before he set her back on the beach. "I am glad you are to be more than a little late!"

She smiled and nodded. "So am I."

Cayden looked to us. "We shall have a celebration this night! There will be bonfires and music and food!"

Xander chuckled. "And you shall weep when the bill comes due, my young friend."

The young dragon lord smiled and shook his head. "I shall never weep again so long as I have Stephanie and our child by my side."

"Very touching is this, but my age is not to be stopping," Abha spoke up.

I glanced at Abha. "How'd you know she was pregnant?"

A sly smile slipped onto the serpent woman's lips. "She is having a greater temperature. Are you not to be seeing how her face is flushed?" I looked to my friend. She was a little more red than usual. "Now if there are no more questions we will be starting the teaching."

Cayden grasped Stephanie's hands and tugged her back toward the house. "Come! We shall celebrate with the finest ice cream!"

Stephanie turned around and waved to us. "Goodbye! See you later!"

I returned the wave, but cringed and lowered my arm when I felt a cold hand on my shoulder. I glanced behind me. It was Lady Abha's hand that gave me the chills. I shakily smiled at her. "So-um, what's on the agenda?"

"The basics of swimming you know, yes?" she asked me.

I shook my head. "Not really. I know just enough to drowned myself."

"I have seen her attempt such an action," Xander spoke up. I shot him a glare.

Abha grabbed my hand and tugged me toward the water. "Then the basics for you I will now be teaching."

"Hey! Wait a sec! I don't have a swimsuit on!" I shouted.

"Your skin is being a good swimsuit," she argued as we tumbled into the water.

I dug into my pocket and whipped my head around. "Look fast, Xander!"

I threw him the small green soul stone given to me by King Thorontur, and he neatly caught it with one hand. He held up his clasped hand and smiled. That didn't give me any comfort as I pushed through the gentle waves. Abha slithered through the gentle, lukewarm waters like a hot knife through butter. I was more like an elephant through a china store. My feet stumbled over the few rocks and bunches of sand until we stopped when the water was waist-height. I yelped when I felt her tail wrap around me.

Abha turned around and slithered the rest of her body back to me. "You must now kick."

I raised an eyebrow. "Why do I-hey-" She yanked me off my feet and I smacked the water with my face.

I flailed my hands and legs for a few seconds before she pulled me back to an upright position. I was hunched forward in her tail with my arms hanging limp in front of me.

She shook her head. "That is not working. You must be kicking. Try again."

My eyes widened and I shook my head. "Don't-" She dunked me into the water.

I kicked and paddled as though my life depended on it. The air in my lungs told me it did. Abha drew me out of the water and I glared at her. "This isn't a swimming lesson. It's a witch trial."

"You are a witch?"

"No."

"Then a trial this is not. We will continue until improvement is seen."

I didn't get a chance to argue before she dropped me again. And again. And again. It was a long morning.

CHAPTER 11

I gargled my way through the rest of the morning until I understood what a drowned rat felt like. I lost count of how many times Abha dunked me, but it was enough that by the time we were finished my lungs burned like a forest fire.

Abha dragged my aching, tired body to the shore and set me down. I kissed the sand, then spit it out. Xander rose from his resting spot on a log and walked over to my sandy spot. He knelt beside me and rubbed my back as he studied my crest-fallen face. "How do you feel?"

I narrowed my eyes at him. "Homicidal."

He chuckled. "I, too, felt very frustrated after my first lesson."

I froze. "*First* lesson? You mean there's more?"

"The swimming you are not doing yet," Lady Abha spoke up as she slithered closer to us. "Though much progress you have made, I cannot say you are swimming yet."

I snorted. "Progress? I didn't swim a single foot."

"It is to your arms we are training. They must have power," she told me.

Xander helped me onto my shaky legs. Gravity was a little different out of the water, and I was exhausted. "I think I'd rather drowned."

She shook her head. "There is no turning back. I have sworn you will be taught, and you will. Lessons will be resumed after lunch. Here you will be being. Good morning." She slithered away back to her small house.

I looked up into Xander's face and put on my best puppy dog eyes. "You're not going to make me come back, are you?"

He smiled and shook his head. "I cannot allow you to quit. You have made good progress this morning, and I am sure you will be able to swim by this afternoon."

I rotated my arm in its socket and winced when a joint popped. "What doesn't kill me makes me stronger?"

He nodded. "Precisely. Now let us to dinner. I am sure you are famished."

I wiggled my finger in my ear to unplug the bay water. "Starving, and a little tired of trying to understand her accent. If she's been teaching so long, why doesn't she know the language?"

"Her forte is swimming, not language, and as a matter of pride the naga consider all other languages inferior to their own, so they give little bother in learning them," he explained.

"So she doesn't want to?"

He smiled. "Precisely. But I believe after all your dunkings you have forgotten something-" He took my hand and set the soul stone in my palm.

I looked at the stone and snorted. "I can't even figure out how to get this thing to work."

Xander grasped my hand and guided me toward the house. "Time will tell what gift king Thorontur has given you, but we will live in the moment, and the moment is dinner."

I glanced around us. "Speaking of we, where's Spiros?"

"He left for the barracks to inform them of the coming ships. We will meet him at the house."

We returned to the house to find Spiros returned and the occupants in a festive mood. Stephanie was seated in the plushest chair in the large living room. She was surrounded on three sides by pillows. Set before her on the coffee table was a large platter of chips, dried fish, and a stack of square blocks of cheese. The expectant father hovered over her as she took a bite from the cheese in her hands.

Darda stood just inside the wide doorway and bowed her head to us as we entered. "Good afternoon, My Lord."

Xander paused by her side and nodded at Cayden. "Has he been in this temperament since their return?"

She smiled and nodded. "Yes, My Lord. He is very concerned for Her Ladyship's health."

Cayden looked up from Stephanie and his face brightened. He strode over and grasped Xander's hand in both of his. "This is wonderful! So very wonderful! I cannot begin to express how wonderful it is to be a father!"

Xander laughed. "I believe you just made a good attempt, though you have some months before you are a father."

"How long does it take for a dragon kid to be born?" I spoke up.

"Six months! Six joyous months!" Cayden told me.

I glanced at Stephanie and snorted. Her stomach bulged a little, but more from the large amount of food than her pregnancy. She wrinkled her nose at the bit of unfinished cheese in her hand and set it on the small plate set before her.

I strode over and slipped one leg over the arm of the chair. "I think your husband's trying to stuff you so he can eat you."

She smiled up at me. "He means well."

I looked to Cayden as he eagerly recounted the joy he was currently feeling. "

Stephanie studied me. "How'd your swimming lesson go?"

I winced and rubbed one of my sore arms. "Let's just say you're lucky you got out of it."

Cayden held up his hands and raised his voice. "Let us to dinner! We shall have a great feast and-" Xander set his hand on the young lord's shoulder.

"We shall celebrate tonight. Miriam will surely drowned if she is weighed down with so much of your generosity."

I raised my hand. "What if I ate just enough to get a stomach ache? Would that get me out of another 'lesson?'"

He chuckled. "I will ensure you do not."

My arm dropped to my side and I drooped. "Damn. . ."

We partook of the meal and I stepped out on the patio alone. Xander remained inside to talk to the excited father-to-be.

I stopped at the end of the patio and looked out over the sea. A gentle breeze rocked the waters and pushed bunches of seaweed onto the shores. I set my hand on my stomach and sighed.

I jumped when a pair of thick arms wrapped themselves around me. Xander set his chin on my shoulder and his eyes studied my face. "Something bothers you."

"Can we still have kids if I'm a fae and a human?" I asked him.

He nodded. "You can."

I cringed. "And if it turns out like that hunchback at Alexandria?"

Xander tightened his grip around me and pressed me close to his chest. "We will hope for the best and pray to the gods that the child is healthy."

I dropped my hand and sighed. "I guess that's all we can do." A sly smile slipped onto my lips as my eyes flickered up to his. "Of course, we could be careful with me and skip these *dangerous* swimming lessons."

He chuckled and shook his head as he slid away from me. "The lessons will continue. Come. Lady Abha no doubt awaits us."

I reluctantly joined Xander for the return trip to the beach. We walked down the stairs to the sand. A familiar piercing noise made me pause. I glanced to our right where most of the docks jutted out into the bay. A few of the local families waded through the waters. I recognized the young boy who I nearly ran down. He splashed in the gentle waves beside a long dock with his mother seated on a lobster trap close by.

Colin picked up a stone and skipped it across the water, and on occasion he would grasp the whistle tied on a string around his neck and blow loud and clear across the bay. He glanced in our direction and waved his whistle in the air. His face was a picture of glee. I waved back and Xander bowed his head.

That reminded me. I drew out the soul stone and held it out to Xander. "You're going to need to hold this again."

He took the stone, but raised his head and looked into the distance with a frown. I followed his gaze. A few other more conspicuous characters wandered over the beach. One was a pig-nosed sus. His small eyes stared at us. He smiled and inclined his head.

Xander did the same before he drew me down the beach. "A friend of yours?" I asked him.

He pursed his lips and shook his head. "I am not acquainted with that sus, but he was very much curious about your soul stone."

I furrowed my brow. "Why? It's just a useless rock. It won't even do anything for me."

"Soul stones are more rare than even Mare Fae. Even without the gift granted by the stone's power, they fetch a great price on the Deep Market," he told me.

I arched an eyebrow. "What's that?"

"A market for ill-gotten goods. One may purchase anything from the poison wrought by witches to slaves kidnapped from the far reaches of the world. You yourself viewed one of its markets in Alexandria, or so Darda told me."

I snorted. "I was a part of it."

His face fell as he studied me. "I am sorry I was not there to protect you."

I shook my head and waved my hand. "It's not your fault. I blame that slimy lizard guy, whatever he was."

"A gamme," he reminded me.

"Are a lot of gamme like him, or are they like the sus?" I asked him.

He pursed his lips as he looked ahead. "It is very nearly in their nature to be so treacherous. The whole of the species is little trusted in our world, and in so being they resort to thieving to earn a living."

I winced. "Sounds like a vicious cycle."

He nodded. "Yes, but let us set aside the darker points of the world and focus on the brighter ones, such as your achieving the ability to swim."

I leaned toward him and fluttered my eyes at my dragon lord. "Or we could just forget the whole thing and find a nice, quiet spot to be alone together."

His face tensed. I had him locked in a Catch-22. Finally he closed his eyes and shook his head. "I cannot allow you to quit."

My shoulders slumped and my lips jutted out in a pout as I turned my face away. "Are we sure I'm a Mare Fae? I don't seem to have any talent for water other than crying healing tears."

He smiled down at me. "I am very grateful you have such an ability."

I couldn't stop the small smile that slipped onto my lips. "It was kind of useful there, wasn't it?"

By this time we reached the northern cliffs. Abha stood waist-deep in the water and beckoned to me. I took a deep breath and waded to her.

My stern coach looked me up and down. "The practicing of you is done. Now you will swim."

I leaned back and blinked at her. "But I haven't even done a stroke."

Her tail wrapped around me. I yelped as she lifted me out of the water and above her head. "You will now be remembering kicking and stroking. Then you will swim."

My eyes widened as she drew me back like a tightening catapult. "Wait! Not ready! Not-" She threw me.

I flailed in the air before I came down in a particularly deep spot. So deep, in fact, that my toes couldn't reach the bottom. Well, unless my head was underwater which is what happened. I hit the water and sank to the bottom. My arms and legs, out of habit from the morning's exercise, kicked and stroked.

A wide, stupid smile widened my face as I found myself propelled through the water. That is, until I realized I traveled sideways. I turned myself in the upward direction and soon broke the surface. Sweet, precious air filled my lungs. I kicked my legs to keep myself above the water and waved my hand to Abha and Xander.

"I did it! I'm swimming!" I yelled.

That's when the siren sounded.

CHAPTER 12

"Keep her in the water!" Xander ordered Abha as he rushed southward down the beach.

I tried to follow him, but Abha swam over and wrapped her body tight around me. I twisted around and pushed against her snake body. "Let me go!"

"You are remaining here," she insisted.

I glared at Xander's disappeared, and cute, backside. "Xander! You ass! Tell her to let me go!" He didn't even pause.

Abha glanced to our left. "He is being careful. Look."

She pointed in the direction of the opening of the bay. I followed her finger and my eyes widened as I beheld a small fleet of white-sailed ships. They drew into the bay on the winds of the ocean and extended their oars once they entered the calm bay. The wooden paddles stretched fifty feet and allowed the ships to cut through the water toward the docks.

I squirmed and thrashed. "Let me go! I want to help!"

She scoffed. "A Mare Fae who is hardly swimming? Are you having any powers?"

I glared at her. "Just let me go! Now!"

My word was punctuated by an unnatural phenomenon. A wave swelled from the deeper depths of the water to our left and slammed into us. The wave slipped between the snake and my body, and pushed us apart. I yelped and took in a mouthful of water as I was dragged down the bay by the rogue wave.

Abha stood in the water and watched me move farther and farther away from her. I waved to her. "Some help here!"

A sly smile slipped onto her lips. She raised her hand and waved back. "You are doing good swimming now!"

"*Not helping!*"

I twisted around in the grip of the wave and watched the beach fly by. Xander had a twenty-yard head start, but I was gaining. Unfortunately, I was also coming between the shore and the incoming ships. Also, there was a problem with the docks. I was coming up on a long one that was too low for me to sail under.

I leaned back and pressed my feet in the water like there was a brake. "Whoa!"

The wave stopped and melted into the water. I was dunked into the six-feet deep water and came up sputtering.

The fast ships reached the docks and a rough-looking crew of monsters jumped onto the planks. Their features were hidden under heavy cloaks made of sheep skin and the skulls covered their faces. Most carried leather bags, but some wielded slingshots. I'd seen enough of Euclid's expertise with that weapon to know it was no toy.

I paddled toward shore. My terrible form meant I sounded like a bull in a china shop. The rough customers on my dock hurried down the planks toward to me. My feet touched land and I sloshed through the water to shore. I was in front of Cayden's beach paradise that was now a hellish war zone.

A ram's horn blown by one of the invaders sounded the alarm and my pursuers paused. Many shouted and pointed to the southern cliffs. Two dozen shadows flew from the barracks toward them. I hurried away from the dock, but the bag-carrying things merely scurried past me onto shore. They rushed up the beach onto the road like rabbits and disappeared into the interior of the land.

The ones with the slingshots knelt on one knee in the direction of the southern cliffs and drew out little balls of a waxy green substance. They armed the sling and drew back the shot. Another row of the invaders with thick wooden shields placed themselves between the weaponed comrades and the incoming dragons.

"Hold your hands!" one of the invaders bellowed.

The fellow wore the largest ram skull among them and stood among the weapon wielders. He raised his hand. The dragons drew closer. Fifty yards. Twenty. He dropped his arm. The slingshot people fired their gunky balls at the dragon warriors. The ammo splatted against the wings and bodies of the dragons. Any who were touched cried out in pain and fell from the sky in a dizzying tailspin. Their wings disappeared into their backs and their taloned claws became human hands. They hit the water hard.

Half of the remaining patrol dove down after them while the other half stopped their charge in midair. They held bows and drew arrows from the quivers on their backs. The dragons fired off the arrows, but the shields blocked most of the arrows.

An errant arrow whistled past me and reminded me I was in a bad spot. I rushed to the stairs and onto the patio. A crashing noise came from inside and the patio doors were flung open. Colin and his mother ran out with one of the invaders close at their heels.

I picked up one of the pillows for the benches and whacked him in the face. The invader was more stunned by the soft attack than the attack himself and stumbled back. A low growl echoed from his skull helmet.

I backed up with my pillow weapon against my chest and nervously smiled at him. "Sorry?"

He let out a yell and lunged at me. A shadow flew down from the roof and slammed into his back. The invader crashed face-first into the hard stone patio flooring. His skull helmet broke in twain and revealed the face of a human man.

I looked up and smiled at Xander. "You're late." He had a stern face as he picked me up and tossed me over his shoulder. "Hey! Lemme down!"

"You were to remain with Abha," he growled as he marched inside the house.

There was a mild amount of destruction in the hall, and I heard a sound of clashing metal come from the kitchen. Colin and his mother hurried behind us.

"Your Lordship, are these the humans who have terrorized the coast?" Colin's mother asked us.

"They are pirates, Mother!" Colin shouted with glee.

"They are indeed the human scavengers," Xander confirmed.

We turned right at the entrance hall and hurried to the kitchen doorway where we stopped. Before us stood Darda, and opposite her was one of the cloaked humans. She held a ladle, he a long sword. They fenced to and fro around the kitchen, overturning pots and pans as they went. The four of us watched like spectators at a tennis match until Xander cleared his throat.

"A moment, My Lord," Darda replied. She disarmed the fellow with a quick twist of her wrist and conked him hard on the head. He dropped to the floor in a heap of sheep rags before she turned to us. "I am glad to see you are both safe."

Xander pursed his lips as he looked down at the unconscious human. "These humans have no killing intent."

I snorted. "They were just after everybody for their clothes?"

He set me down. "That is quite possible, but for now you must remain here while I fend them off."

I crossed my arms and glared at him. "Like hell I am. I'm going with you."

"Me, too!" Colin yelled.

His mother grabbed his shoulders and pulled him against her chest. "You are certainly not!"

"There will be no discussions," Xander replied as he looked to Darda. "Keep her inside." Darda bowed her head.

Xander turned away. I reached out for his arm, but Darda leapt between us and shook her head. "Let him be, Miriam."

I frowned. "I can help!"

She arched an eyebrow. "How do you intend to do so?"

I grabbed a spoon off the island and waved it at her. "I don't care. I'll fight with this if I-" Darda knocked the spoon out of my hand with her ladle.

"You would only endanger both of you," she insisted.

I whipped my head around for another weapon. A pitcher of water sat on the counter. I rushed over and picked it up. The water sloshed over me as I spun around to face Darda. "I can control water!"

She furrowed her brow. "Miriam, have you lost your senses?"

"I can! Watch!" I concentrated on the surface. My reflection glared back at me. After a few moments I relaxed and frowned. "I know I can."

Darda walked over to me and set a hand on my shoulder. "I will protect you here. Be assured of-" I whacked her arm away.

"I don't want protecting! I've had enough of everybody pulling me around like I'm some dead weight!" I snapped. I stuck my arm in the pitcher to draw water. "I'm going to do something!"

And I did. The water in the pitcher rose up in the shape of a serpent and hissed at Darda. She stumbled back with her mouth agape. Colin's mother drew him back, but he grinned and pointed at the creature. "I want one of those, Mother!"

I gawked at the serpent. "Am I...am I doing that?"

Darda set her eyes on me and blinked. "My Lady, how have you done that?"

OCEANS BENEATH DRAGONS

I shook my head as I drew my arm from the water. The sea dragon shrank in size. I pushed my arm back in and it got bigger. An idea hit me. I stiffened my jaw and shoved the jar into Darda's hands. The ladle clattered to the floor. "Stay here and protect these two."

"But Miriam-" Darda started as I strode past her.

I took off and my voice echoed behind me. "If this works I'll be right back!"

CHAPTER 13

I raced down the hall and out onto the patio. The beach was a war zone. Soldiers in armor dragged their brethren from the water. Others still in flight shot arrows at the slingshot men. Invaders came over the small hill onto the beach. In front of them were small flocks of bleating sheep that they herded onto the docks. Xander stood chest-deep in the bay two dozen yards from the right side of the battle-line dock hauling the unconscious bodies of dragon warriors from the waters.

I jumped down the stairs and raced down the beach to the water where I splashed into the cool bay. A few stray arrows dropped into the water some five yards from me. I pushed through the water until I was chest deep. The boats rocked the bay with small waves.

OCEANS BENEATH DRAGONS

I stuck my arms into the water and bit my lip. "I hope this does something. . ." Nothing happened. The waters remained calm. Some of the invaders glanced in my direction. I glared at the water. "We don't have all day!"

The water around me gurgled. A long form burst from the surface and stretched twenty feet into the air. It was the same serpent from the pot, but this one was ten times as large. It reared its head and let loose a cry that echoed down the beach. Attackers and defenders pause and turned to see what was the commotion. Many mouths dropped open that day.

Half the men with slingshots turned and fired at my serpent. Their gunky balls hit the surface and dropped harmlessly into the water in front of me. The creature hissed and charged. At the last moment before it hit the dock it turned. A tail flew out of the water and knocked the men off the dock and into the water.

The horn sounded. "Aboard! Aboard!" Big-Skull called.

The men on the beach sounded their trumpets. Invaders crested the short hill behind the beach. Ahead of them were small flocks of sheep and the occasional cow. The men with the catapults let loose a thick volley that covered their companions as the animals were herded onto the dock and onto the ships. My victims swam to the boats and were helped aboard.

I turned my dragon toward the rear boats. Some of the catapults were turned toward me. They fired some of their heavy clods at me. The mud whistled through the air and splattered around me, covering me in bits of the slimy substance. I sloshed and pushed through the water in order to avoid the mucky projectiles. One of the balls grazed my forehead. I stumbled to one side as the world spun around me. My hands lost contact with the water as I clutched my head. The water dragon disappeared.

A whistling noise approached me. One of the balls arched down toward my head. I threw up my arms, shut my eyes and braced for impact.

A winged shadow flew in front of me. I felt strong arms wrap around me and use their body to push me away. I opened my eyes and watched as Xander was hit in the side by the glob of goop. His face scrunched up in pain. He slipped behind me and crashed landed in the water. I spun around and saw his wings shrivel into his back. The gunk was washed from his side, but he didn't stir. His twisted face partially floated above the surface before he slowly sank into the water.

"Xander!" I shouted.

I lunged at him and looped my arms under his armpits. Even without his wings he was heavy, but the buoyancy of the water helped me pull him toward shore. Another loud, long horn sounded. I paused and looked out at the bay. The invader ships pushed away from the docks and unfurled their white sails. They sailed across the bay and out of the mouth.

No one followed them. There were few left of the dragon men who still had their wings, and all the others helped heft their comrades to the beaches.

"Miriam!" I returned my attention to the shores. Spiros stumbled through the waves toward me. Spiros reached me and slung one of Xander's arms across his shoulders, lifting my burden. "Follow me."

Spiros pulled Xander to the beach where he laid the dragon lord on the white sands. His face was hardly more colorful. I dropped to my knees beside Xander.

"Xander?" He didn't reply. I shook his shoulders. His head lolled to one side. "Xander! Come on, Xander! Wake up! Please wake up!"

Spiros knelt beside me and gently pushed me to the side. "Let me see him."

I scuttled out of the way and watched as Spiros set his hand on Xander's chest over his heart. Spiros pursed his lips before he dropped his hand and looked to me. "Does your shoulder hurt?"

I blinked at him. "My-"

"Does your Mark hurt?" he rephrased.

I shook my head. "N-no, why?"

His tense expression relaxed. "Then we have nothing to fear. His heart is normal, and if you sense nothing than he is not in danger."

I set my hand on my shoulder. I'd forgotten about the Mark Darda had bestowed on me that fateful first adventure.

Speaking of Darda. "Miriam!"

I looked up and watched Darda scuttle across the sands with Cayden catching and passing her. Cayden arrived at us and his eyes widened as he beheld Xander's still figure. He whipped his head to Spiros. "Is he-?"

Spiros shook his head. "No. He was merely hit by the Dragon Bane."

Cayden ran a hand through his hair. "Thank goodness."

Stephanie knelt beside me and set her hands on my shoulders as she looked into my face. "Are you okay?"

I pursed my lips, but nodded. "Yeah. At least, I think so."

"Was it you who made that water dragon?" she asked me.

I raised my hands and looked at the dripping, pruned fingers. "Yeah, but don't ask me to tell you how I did it."

"Your Mare Fae blood allowed you to control the waters, Miriam," Darda reminded me.

"We should return to the house," Spiros advised as he lifted Xander's limp body into his arms.

Cayden glanced at the beach. Dozens of men were sprawled on the white sands. All were unconscious while their comrades attended to them. Lady Abha slipped among them dispensing dampened towels from a bowl that the men used to wipe away any remainder of the mud. "I will join you shortly. I must see to my men."

Stephanie took a step toward him. "Let me go with you."

He returned his attention to her and shook his head. "No. You must also return to the house."

She furrowed her brow. "But I-"

He grasped her hands and smiled into her concerned eyes. "The danger is past, but I would rather you and our child returned to the house."

Stephanie's head drooped, but she nodded. Cayden pecked a light kiss on her forehead and hurried away. Our little group returned to the house where Darda and I followed Spiros upstairs to the bedroom I shared with Xander.

Spiros gently laid him on the bed and opened his shirt to inspect his side. There was a round red mark like a rash where the mud had hit him.

I looked up at Spiros's tense face. "The Dragon Bane isn't permanent, right?"

He set Xander's shirt back down and shook his head. "So little is known of the substance, but all previous cases were cured by a fortnight of rest. However-" he turned his head and caught my eyes, "-none of the other affected were dragon lords."

The color drained from my face. "What's that mean?"

"The dragon lords are different from others of our kind in that they are closer to our dragon ancestors than any other line," he explained. He glanced down at Xander and studied the lord's quiet countenance. "The Bane attacks the dragon blood within us. For one who's blood is closer to that of a dragon than our human forms, only time will tell us how the concoction will effect him."

I grasped one of Xander's hands in both of mine and studied Xander's face with pursed lips. "Why'd you have to go and be a big hero?"

"My promise demanded it." We all started back at the soft sound of Xander's voice. His eyes fluttered open and he turned his head toward me to give me a weak smile as his hand gently squeezed mine. "I will not allow any more harm to come to you."

Tears leapt into my eyes, but they weren't from relief. I put my free hand on my hip and glared down at him. "That gunk doesn't hurt me, remember? For all we know it could have killed you!"

His eyes flickered down his body. "But I remain alive, and there was a risk for you, as well."

I blinked at him. "What risk?"

He studied my face with pursed lips. "You are hardly more human than I, and though the weapon is called Dragon Bane, we know not what its effects are on one with the lineage of a fae."

My anger fled and my shoulders slumped. I sighed and ran a hand through my hair. "Why do you have to make sense so much?"

Xander smiled at me. "One of us must be sensible."

My eyes narrowed. "You're skating on pretty thin ice for a dragon who can't fly for a while."

Xander shifted atop the bed and winced. He held up his free hand and focused hard on the fingers. Nothing happened, and after a moment he dropped the hand back on the bed. "So it seems. Even my claws will not heed my command to show themselves."

At that moment Cayden and Stephanie entered the room. Their tense faces were relieved by the sight of Xander's wakefulness, and Cayden moved to stand on the other side of the bed as Spiros stepped away from the bed. "How do you feel?"

Xander smiled at his old friend. "As though a herd of ?? ad trampled me, but how are your men and your people?"

"They are all well thanks to your help." Cayden looked to me and his eyes fell on my hands. "How did you come to create the sea serpent?"

I shrugged. "I don't know. I just kind of stuck my hands in water and it popped out."

"The longer you remain in our world, the greater your fae strength may become," Spiros spoke up.

Cayden bowed his head to we three. "In any case, I am grateful for your assistance, and bring better news. My flagship has arrived. I mean to follow the raiders and confirm the source as being that of the island."

OCEANS BENEATH DRAGONS

I noticed Stephanie's face paled a little. She set a hand on his arm and looked into his face. Her voice was small and quivering. "Must you?"

He looked to her and nodded. "I must. These raids must be stopped before someone is killed."

Spiros arched an eyebrow. "No one was killed during this raid?"

Cayden shook his head. "No. By the grace of the gods, everyone was spared, but we cannot lean on their graces forever. I intend to find the source of the troubles and stop them ."

"And I will come with you," Xander spoke up as he raised himself up on his shaky arms.

Spiros and Darda stepped forward while I grabbed his shoulders and stopped him from rising. "Like hell you are! You're staying right here and recuperating!"

"She is correct, My Lord. You must not exert yourself during your infirmity," Darda added.

Spiros stepped up to the foot of the bed and bowed his head. "If you will allow me, I will go in your place."

"I have no need for a replacement," Xander insisted as he pushed against my hands.

I pursed my lips and leaned my weight into a shove that pushed him back against the pillows. My success surprised us both as we stared in shock at each other. I pointed a finger at my chest. "Did I just beat you?"

"In your condition you are no match even for the strength of Miriam," Spiros pointed out.

I whipped my head to him and narrowed my eyes. "What's that supposed to mean?"

"It means in a battle he would be killed," Cayden spoke up.

"Then as the most senior warrior I will go with you to observe and advise," Xander insisted.

I glared at him. "If you're going, then so am I."

He shook his head. "I cannot allow that. As a human-"

"That just beat your butt in a test of strength, I'm going with you," I finished for him.

"Then I will go as well," Spiros spoke up.

Cayden pursed his lips, but turned to Darda. "Will you at least remain with Stephanie and my child to protect them?"

She bowed her head. "It would be an honor."

I grinned. "Then it's settled. We leave tomorrow."

CHAPTER 14

My bold words came back to bite me in the ass. Tomorrow came early. *Really* early. The sun wasn't even thinking about rising when I was aroused from my sleep on the bed. My eyes fluttered open. A large, familiar shadow loomed over me. It was Darda.

"Wake up, Miriam! The ship is about to launch!" she warned me.

My eyes shot open and I shot up. I whipped my head to the spot beside me. It was empty. I whipped my head back to Darda and got a little whiplash. "Where's Xander?"

She grabbed my arm and tugged me out of bed. "Aboard the ship! Now you must hurry or you will be left behind!"

"*What?*"

My feet hit the floor and I leapt over to the dresser. Darda was close behind me. I hopped into my pants as she drew out my shirt. My hops were in time with my words. "How could he do this to me? He said I could go!"

"He did not explicitly give his permission," she pointed out.

I snatched the shirt from Darda and glared at her. "He still doesn't have to leave me behind!"

I dashed from the room and pulled my shirt on during my flight down the stairs. The house was dark and quiet. A few candles flickered in the entrance hall. Fog drifted past the windows. I grabbed the bottom post of the stairs and swung around so I was in the central hallway. The double doors to the rear patio were open. Stephanie stood at the railing with her eyes on the two small away-boats that were docked at the long, mist-shrouded dock. They were shoving off for the large clump of lights beyond the mouth of the foggy bay. Cayden's warship awaited them.

I was going to make sure it awaited me, too.

I pounded down the hall and out onto the patio. Stephanie turned and her eyes widened. "Xander said you weren't feeling well."

I flew down the stairs and onto the beach. The fog parted for my drop. "*He's* the one who's going to need a doctor!" I shouted back over my shoulder as I raced across the sand.

The strong crew of the away-boats sailed past the end of the dock and out into the open waters of the bay. I skidded to a stop at the end of the pier and glared at the dark figures seated in the two boats. One of them turned at my coming and I recognized that handsome face.

"Bingo. . ." I murmured.

OCEANS BENEATH DRAGONS

I knelt down and stuck my hands in the water. The surface gurgled and frothed. My sea dragon exploded from the depths of the bay and stretched into the dark, early-morning sky. Its long neck hovered close to me. I slowly stood and tapped my foot against the water beast's back. It was solid.

Only the lamps at the bows of the away-boats told me where they were, the mouth of the bay. I took a deep breath and, careful not to loose water contact, leapt onto the creature's back. There was a little give, but I was buoyed by a saddle that rose from its watery body. My hands now clutched a set of reins.

"Come on, boy!" I yelled to my creation as I turned us toward the mouth of the bay.

The creature turned at my command and cut through the water like a hot knife through margarine. The boats had hardly reached the ship when I broke through the entrance to the bay and sailed toward them. The crew aboard ship loomed out of the fog and raced to the starboard railing to watch me.

I grinned and pulled back on the reins. The reins didn't pull back with me, and I found myself empty-handed. I was also empty-dragoned. The sea serpent beneath me disappeared faster than I could say 'shit,' or even take a breath of air before I dropped into the cold water of the open ocean.

I kicked my feet and broke through the surface. A large wave splashed over me and shoved me back down into the chilling waters. A shadow sailed over me, a long arm was shoved into the water, and I felt my collar grabbed. I was pulled from the ocean and dropped onto the floor of one of the away-boats. My body shivered against the cold wind of the open ocean. A heavy coat was draped over my quivering form and I looked up at the kind soul.

Xander loomed over me with his eyebrows pointed down in a sharp 'V' formation. "Have you no sense?" he scolded me.

I glared back at him. "I-I said I w-was coming."

Beside Xander on the board sat Spiros. "My Lord, the ship."

Xander glanced over his shoulder. The large hull of the warship rose before us. A rope ladder was tossed over the side and reached our small boat. We docked against the side and Xander looked to Spiros. "You will need to carry her, but not gently."

Spiros bowed his head and leaned forward. He looped one arm around me and hefted me over his shoulder. "H-hey! I c-can get-"

"You can hardly speak, much less climb a ladder," Xander pointed out.

I glared at him, but resigned myself to being carried up the rope ladder by Xander's general. He stepped onto the deck and strode to the half front of the ship. A small, short wall of wooden boxes lined the deck, and he set me atop one of the crates.

Xander followed us and knelt in front of me. He readjusted his coat that covered me so warmly as a chill breeze wafted over his own unprotected torso. "You would do well to avoid using your fae abilities in public," he warned me.

I arched an eyebrow between shivers. "W-why? Will it d-drain my life energy or something?"

Xander's eyes met mine. "I do not know, but the attention you draw upon yourself is not wise."

I frowned. "Why not? I thought f-fae were supposed to b-be some sort of gods."

He glanced over his shoulder and swept his eyes over the large deck. Some of the crew hefted the away-boats to the deck. Others scurried about manning the large white sails. More than one pair of eyes glanced in our direction, and some of those glances didn't look friendly.

"Not everyone worships the same god."

Cayden walked over to us, and at his side was a cleanly-cut bearded man in a white sailor's uniform. A large hat that looked like a half circle was perched atop his head. He had a stiff stance and when they stopped in front of us he clasped his hands behind his back and stood as straight as the masts.

Cayden looked to us, but gestured to the stranger. "Lord Xander, Miriam, Spiros, may I introduce you to Captain Grimur Kamban. Captain, Lord Xander, his Maiden Miriam, and his personal guard, Spiros."

The captain stiffly bowed his head. "It is an honor to meet you, Your Lordship, and your companions."

Xander smiled. "Your reputation precedes you, Captain Kamban. I have heard much of your exploits on the seas from Captain Magnus."

Captain Kamban pursed his lips and, if possible, he stiffened even more. I wondered if rigor mortis had set in until he spoke. "I can imagine."

"I believe you once hunted your countryman on these very seas," Xander mused.

The captain nodded. "Yes, and I may promise you that should he leave your service I will venture to try again."

Xander bowed his head. "I will carry your promise to him when I see him again."

Cayden cleared his throat and turned to Kamban. "How long is the journey to the island, captain?"

"We should arrive at the port an hour after sunrise," he replied.

"Then that would give us four hours to deliberate our approach to the humans," Cayden mused.

"We would do better to move the conference to the captain's quarters," Xander added as he climbed to his feet.

I stood with him, but Xander lay his hand on my shoulder and pressed me back down to my hard seat. "You will do better to remain on the deck until we return."

I glared at him. "But you're dealing with humans, so who better to help with the planning than a human?"

"Your affinity for your own kind is admirable, but may not be appreciated," he argued.

That ruffled my feathers. "What's wrong with that?"

The others of our group waited a few steps off. Xander turned to them and nodded in the direction of the cabin. "I will join you in a moment."

Cayden bowed his head, and he and the captain continued forward. Spiros stayed close by while Xander resumed his seat beside me. He clasped our hands together and looked into my eyes with a gentle gaze. "While all aboard this vessel understand that you are my Maiden, many of them have comrades who have been struck by the Dragon's Bane. Because of those familial strikes, and the plunder to the realm they call home, they have little kindness for humans. If you were to lend your voice to the deliberations they would see any plan that materialized as tainted with human bias."

My eyebrows crashed down. "But I didn't do anything to them!"

OCEANS BENEATH DRAGONS

He squeezed my hands and a ghost of a smile slipped across his lips. "I know your nature, but in these moments of tension when the drums of war beat in the distance we must walk a line of diplomacy with both sides. At the moment that side is dragon. Perhaps later this day it will be human, but until that moment arrives we must defend Cayden's people."

I pursed my lips, but my shoulders fell and my head drooped. "All right. . ." I mumbled.

He leaned forward and pecked a kiss on my forehead. "Warm yourself in my coat. I will return as soon as I can."

He stood. His fingers slipped out of mine and my hands dropped into my lap. I looked away as the dragon men turned from me and strode away to the cabin. I was alone.

Or was I?

"Can ya make the Call?"

CHAPTER 15

I started back and whipped my head to my right. A shriveled man with a spry gait and piercing blue eyes stood a foot behind me. He was dressed in brown pants torn above the knees and a shirt that might have been white in some past life but was now a discolored yellow. Atop his wispy white tufts of hair was a cap that looked older than Xander's real age.

There was nothing very unusual about him, but the hairs on the back of my neck stood on end.

I pointed at myself. "Are you talking to me?"

He grinned and showed off an impressive set of decayed chompers. "Who else would I be talkin' to but a fae?"

A chill breeze blew over me and reminded me of my wet blunder. I shivered and wrapped the coat closer to myself as I looked away from the old man. "I don't think I'm much of a fae." I glanced in the direction Xander had gone. The heavy fog obscured the route. "Or even a human."

The man stopped near my side and hunched over to peer at me with his unblinking gaze. "But ya can hear the call, can't ya?" he persisted.

I twisted my head around and glared up at him. "I'm getting really tired of all this cryptic fae stuff. What the hell is-" I lifted my hands and made air quotes, "-the Call?"

He grinned and showed off a set of teeth that would have made a scream and run away. "Yer a sprightly one, aren't ya? I've seen many like ya, but none so quick with a snap."

I turned away and huddled deeper into the coat. "Whatever you're trying to sell, I'm not interested."

He plopped himself beside me like we were old friends. A cold chill swept over me and I scooted a little away from him. He leaned toward to make up for the space.

"An old sea dragon like me hasn't got much to sell, Lady Fae, but what we've learned these long years on the seas. Fer yer question-" he nodded in the direction of the starboard side, "-the Call is what brings 'em out of the deeps."

I followed his gaze and wrinkled my nose. "Brings who out of what?"

He leaned forward at an angle and studied me. I leaned back to escape the dreadful smell that wafted from his decayed mouth. "The deeps are where the Mare Fae came from a long time ago, and where Valtameri has his court."

My ears perked up at the name and I turned my face to the old man. "Valtameri? The guy who runs the oceans?"

The man nodded. "The very same. If ya know the Call ya might be able to bring his offspring, but a good, strong Call might be enough to bring the old king 'imself."

I arched an eyebrow. "So what does this Call sound like?"

He chuckled. "If I knew that, Lady Fae, I wouldn't be talkin' to ya right now." He tapped his elbow against my arm and gave a wink. "I'd be havin' myself a little bit of fun with one of the daughters of ol' Valtameri, if ya know what I mean."

"And you thought I'd know it because I'm a fae?" I guessed.

He nodded. "Aye, but even if ya don't know it I'd bet my last fish ya can *feel* it." He tapped my chest over my heart with one of his bony fingers. "Just there. It beats inside ya like the beating of yer heart." He creaked onto his small feet and bowed his head to me. "I hope to be seeing ya, Lady Fae." He shuffled off down the deck and disappeared behind another pile of crates.

My curiosity was piqued by the strange men, so much so that I stood and followed him behind the crates. There was no sign of the old man, but there were two other sailors, a young man and a middle-aged one. They looked up from their rope wrapping. One of them glared at me.

"What's wanted?" he snapped.

"Did you see an old guy pass by here a second ago?" I asked him.

He shook his head. "No, and we wouldn't. There's no old sailors aboard Lord Cayden's flagship."

My eyebrows crashed down. "Then how was I just talking to one a minute ago?"

One of the sailors lifted his head and his eyes widened. The gruff one sneered at me. "I'd say you were seeing things in the fog, miss. Now if ya don't mind we'll be getting back to our work." He lowered his head and resumed the rope wrapping.

I pursed my lips, but turned and returned to my crate. My eyes followed the path I'd seen the old man disappear. I was sure he'd gone that way, but the one sailor had said there shouldn't even be an old guy aboard.

As I was looking at the other line of crates one of the sailors appeared. It was the less sneering, younger man. He kept looking over his shoulder as he crept up to me, and he spoke in a hushed whisper. "Did you really see an old man aboard?" he asked me.

I arched an eyebrow, but nodded. "Yeah, why?"

"What'd he look like?"

I shrugged. "He was dressed in a pair of old brown pants and a shirt. Why?"

"What was the color of his eyes?"

I leaned back and frowned at the fellow. "Why do you want to know?"

He gave another glance over his shoulder before he dared take a seat beside me. "I think I might know who you saw. My dad-he was a sailor, too-he used to tell me stories about an old man of the ocean who'd sometimes appear on a ship. He was supposed to be the ghost of a shipwrecked who'd come aboard and talk to some of the crew and passengers."

I shivered and wrapped the coat closer around me. "So is this some ill-omen of imminent doom or what?"

He shook his head. "My dad said he was supposed to bring good luck to the ship's journey-"

"Hey! Where'd ya go?" I heard the gruff sailor call out through the fog.

The younger one by my side jumped to his feet. "I gotta go."

I grabbed his sleeve. "Wait a sec. If that guy was a ghost why'd he talk to me?"

He shrugged. "I don't know, but I gotta go."

The sailor pulled from my grasp and hurried away into the fog. I was left with the sinking feeling that I'd been talking to a dead guy. My eyes flitted over the foggy deck. The area was empty, but I could hear the calls of the sailors as they went about their work.

"Good luck, huh?" I murmured as I wrapped the coat closer to myself. A sneeze interrupted my thoughts. I rubbed my nose with my finger. "He'd better start with the good luck before I die of pneumonia."

Even a visit with a ghost couldn't shake the fatigue from my weary bones. I dozed off and was awakened by a soft shake of my shoulder. My eyes fluttered open. Before me stood Xander. Behind him was the whole of the deck. The fog was gone, and the pink color of nearly-dawn shown over the sails.

I sat up and winced as my back complained about my rough bed of crates. "Done deciding the fate of humans?"

He took a seat beside me and pursed his lips. "There was less to deliberate than to learn."

I rubbed some of the sleep from my eyes. "Come again?"

"Cayden and Captain Kamban told me of what they knew about the island of Ui Breasail and its inhabitants."

"And?"

He leaned back against the crates and pursed his lips as he looked ahead of us. "If negotiations fail, there will be war."

My shoulders drooped. "Seriously?"

He nodded. "Unfortunately, yes. The people of Ui Breasail are very proud, and pride may make them unwilling to negotiate. They also have the upper hand should war be the only option. The island is a natural fortress surrounded by rocks but for one large cove. With their control of the cove and Dragon's Bane they would be impossible to overcome by sea and nearly the same by air."

Sunrise was nearly upon us, and the growing light allowed me to study his pensive face with its dark shadows. "You look tired."

A weary smile slipped onto his lips and he tilted his head to look at me. "I do not know how you can do it."

I blinked at him. "Do what?"

"Be a human." He raised one hand and studied the fingers. "You have such frail bodies and minimal strength, and yet even in this world where war and competition have brought the species to the brink of extinction your kind continues to persevere."

I wrapped my arm around his shoulders and grinned. "We're a pretty stubborn race."

He returned my grin with a broadened smile. "So you have taught me. Try as I might you insist on testing my ability to protect you."

"Maybe I'll be the one to protect you this time. Besides, I've got a guardian ghost on my side."

He blinked at me. "Pardon?"

"Land ho!"

CHAPTER 16

We leapt to our feet. The rising sun peeked over the horizon and bathed us in its bright light. Cayden and Spiros made their appearance from the cabin at the back of the ship.

"Ui Breasail has been sighted," Cayden informed us as he nodded behind and to our left.

Xander and I turned around and beheld a green sight. The island of Ui Breasail was a long stretch of land covered in a thick green forest of tall trees. The canopy stretched two hundred feet into the air and draped the soil beneath it in deep shadows. The coast of the island was dotted with large gray rocks that stuck out of the water like jagged teeth on a sleeping giant.

"Where's the cove?" I asked him.

"On the far side of the island. It is one of the many reasons no one has ever made a successful sea invasion," he told me.

Our ship sailed around the southern tip some ten miles down and we traveled across the breadth of the island. The land stretched another ten miles before we reached the opposite shore. The island curved outward in an arc where the sides were dotted with the rocks. A narrow opening led into a cove of steep cliffs not unlike those of the Bay of Secrets.

A long wooden dock stretched from the shore and some hundred feet into the bay. Two long columns of marauders stood on the dock. They all wore the sheep skulls and held spears. At the head of the columns and the dock stood the leader of the raiding party, the man with the ram skull. Beside him was a more normal looking-and handsome-fellow who stood a head taller than the burly others. A sash was draped from his shoulder across his chest to his waist and behind him.

Xander tensed by my side. He hurried to the left side of the ship and stared intently at the men at the end of the dock. I joined him and looked from the dock to his tense face. "What's wrong?"

He pressed his lips so tightly together the color drained from them. "That man out there."

I looked back to the man beside ram-skull head. "What about him?"

Spiros came up on Xander's other side and surveyed the welcome party. His eyebrows crashed down. "He has a red sash, Xander."

I glanced from one to the other. "What's that mean? Who is he?"

"His bearing shows he is not a human, and he wears the color of the Bestia Draconis," Xander told me.

The tension aboard ship tightened as we approached this unwelcome party. Captain Kamban stood on raised platform at the back of the ship and behind the wheel. His booming voice quailed the quivering of his crew. "Let up the sails! Lower the anchor!"

The men jumped at his barking commands. The sails were shut and the anchor lowered. The ship stopped at the mouth of the cove. The crew prepared two of the away-boats.

Xander half-turned to Spiros. "You will go with Miriam in a separate boat." Spiros bowed his head.

I frowned. "What? Why can't I go with you?"

"Because I cannot protect you against a dragon," he pointed out.

Cayden and Xander piled into a separate away-boat than Spiros and I. The other spaces were taken up by the burliest of the ship's crew. They carried with them a wide assortment of small weapons hidden inside the coats of their uniforms.

The boats sped through the waters of the calm bay, but stopped fifty feet from the tip of the dock. There was no place to dock without tossing the rope at the long line of armed men.

Cayden stood in his boat. "We come with open arms, human."

"And weapons in your coats," called back the ram-headed man.

"Surely you would not begrudge us some protection against the Dragon's Bane," Cayden argued.

OCEANS BENEATH DRAGONS

The human looked over the burly men in the boats. His brief perusal paused on me. "Are there women now on your ships?"

Cayden gestured to me. "She is a sign that we mean no harm, and only wish to speak with you."

The leader of the skull men deliberated for a moment before he glanced over his shoulder. He gave a nod, and the lines behind him turned and retreated from the dock. The human returned his attention to us. "You may come ashore, but be warned we will not hesitate to use what you call 'Dragon's Bane' on you."

Cayden bowed his head. "We are grateful for your invitation."

Our boats were pulled on either side of the dock and the rope grabbed by a few of the humans. I stepped onto the dock and watched as the the tall gentleman beside the human stepped up before Xander. Xander stiffened and set his hand on the hilt of Bucephalus, but the man smiled and bowed his head. "It is an honor to meet Ferus Draco."

Xander's face darkened. "The honor is yours alone."

A strange twinkle slipped into the stranger's eyes. "I am sorry you feel that way, *false Grand Dragon Lord.*"

Xander unsheathed Bucephalus and took a step toward the other dragon. Cayden and Spiros grabbed either of his shoulders and held him back as the stranger backed away. When Xander spoke his voice was a hiss filled with venom. "The only false dragon is one who wears that sash."

"Xander, mind yourself," Spiros whispered to him.

The ram-headed man stepped up to the tense crowd and frowned as he looked between the two opposing groups. "I will not have dragons fight among themselves on my island. If you wish to kill each other, then do it elsewhere."

Xander relaxed, and his two compatriots released him. My dragon lord sheathed his sword, turned to the human and bowed his head. "My apologies. I meant no disrespect to you."

The human scoffed. "Likely not, but another mistake like that and I will have you thrown into the breakwaters that surround this island." His eyes flickered to the red dragon. "That goes for both of you."

The stranger smiled, but bowed his head. "I understand."

"Then follow me," the human commanded as he turned away from us.

A few sailors remained with the away-boats, but a dozen of us followed the ram-headed man down the dock and onto the island. The guards from the dock stood on either side of a rock-stepped path that led into the thick foliage of the island. Women, men without dead animal skulls, and children watches from behind the line of guards. Much of their clothing was created from light wool, and their tanned gave them a leathery appearance. They peered curiously at us as we traveled past. I was a half a head shorter than many of the guards, so I got a glimpse of arm hair and a few children who peeked out from between legs.

One viewer, however, caught my attention. The figure was a young girl of sixteen. She was hunched over on one of the high branches of a tall tree and watched us with open curiosity. Her attire was a short woolen dress as light as a floating cotton blossom. She wore her long brown hair down her back in a single braid, and her blue eyes stood out from among the other brown ones that stared at us.

We turned a bend in the path and I lost sight of her. The ram-headed man led us deep into the thick forest of maple-like trees and thick bushes with sharp thorns. The air was humid, but not enough to stifle my unprepared lungs.

After a mile the path widened and the rough rocks fell away to be replaced by square stones notched expertly together. We climbed a short hill and the trees parted to reveal a small valley below us. My eyes widened as I beheld a majestic city of stone nestled in the greenery of valley.

The city was hewn from a white, glistening stone that seemed to sink into the valley. The layout of the metropolis was circular and divided into terraces. The outer terraces were the highest up the valley walls, and each successive interior terrace sat lower in the valley. Tall and short walls separated the terraces, and stone stairs connected them.

In the very center of the city arose a round domed building that stretched a hundred feet into the sky. A few smaller domed buildings dotted the outer rings of the city.

The ram-skull man led us down the hill along white stone steps to the top of the first terrace. I paused atop the hill and furrowed my brow. "Does that kind of look like a ball of wool?"

Cayden stepped up beside me and nodded. "They owe much of their prosperity to their sheep."

We continued onward with the group and reached the outskirts of the city. It was a metropolis of some five thousand souls. Not on par with Alexandria, but larger than I expected the human habitation to be. Many of the homes were two floors, and green vines, flowers and trees decorated their white walls. The notches in the stone houses were like those of the streets. I pushed against a crumbling stone wall around a small yard. The stone didn't give an inch.

We traveled down to the center of the city. The inhabitants gathered around the side streets to watch the procession of guards and we strangers. None of them had blue eyes.

The procession reached the last terrace with its domed building. A garden of colorful flowers surrounded its perimeter. The arched entranceway was covered by a portico, and inside was a wide hall with smaller offshoots. The ceiling rose above our heads some fifty feet and on the white surface was painted scenes of pastoral paradise. The columns on either side of us were topped with stone balls in the shape of wool, and little stone sheep played among them.

We headed straight and soon arrived in the center of the building. A pair of heavy wooden doors were opened for us, and beyond them was a circular room. In the center of the room was a throne atop a five-foot tall pedestal. On the woolen cushion of the throne sat a wreath made of gold.

The two columns of guards circled either side of the room and stood at attention facing the center. The red dragon walked over to stand close to the bottom of the pedestal.

The ram-skulled man strode up to the pedestal and walked the few steps up to the throne. The man turned to us and removed the skull. He was about fifty with brown hair grayed at the temples. His face was weathered by sun and time, but his eyes were as sharp as those of an eagle as he looked down at us. He set the skull on the floor by his feet and crowned himself with the wreath before he took a seat.

"Now what would you speak of with me, Cathal, high king of Ui Breasail?"

CHAPTER 17

Cayden stepped to the front of our group and knelt on one knee before the ram-skull king. "A moment, if you would, Your Highness. We would like to ask a great favor of you before we begin these negotiations."

The king arched an eyebrow. "And what is that?"

"We ask only that during our visit none of your ships will leave the island," Cayden requested.

The human scoffed. "We must fish for what little catch these waters offer us."

Cayden smiled. "My apologies. Only that they not raid the coast, and if they are out that they will return."

King Cathal studied Cayden for a moment with pursed his lips before he nodded. "I swear to you on my honor that none of our ships are away from the island, nor will they leave for the coast until we have spoken."

Cayden bowed his head. "I will accept your word, Your Highness, and thank you for your kindness."

The king scoffed. "It is not kindness but annoyance that grants you your wish. I wish for you to be gone as quickly as possible."

Cayden climbed to his feet and tilted his head up to look the king in the eyes. "We would like nothing better ourselves, King Cathal, but first I demand to know why you invade my realm and steal away my people's goods."

"Necessity knows nothing about stealing," King Cathal argued.

Cayden gestured to the guards in their woolen clothes and skulls. "But your island is legendary for its flocks of sheep. Why must you steal our animals?"

The king stiffened and pursed his lips. "It is because we ourselves have been violated that we seek to lessen the suffering of my people with these voyages."

The young dragon lord arched an eyebrow. "But how is that possible? How can anyone violate your impenetrable defenses?"

Cathal shifted in his seat and furrowed his brow. "We do not know, but with each passing day our flocks grow smaller. That is why we venture forth."

"But suffering should not be met with more suffering," Cayden argued. He took a step toward the king. The guards around us stiffened. "Your Highness, for the sake of both our realms your raids must stop."

Cathal frowned. "While my people suffer, the raids will continue. That is-" a sly smile slipped onto his lips as he leaned back to study Cayden, "-unless you wish to offer some 'compensation' in return for an end to these raids."

OCEANS BENEATH DRAGONS

"What?" I yelped. My voice bounced against the walls and echoed back at me, amplified a thousand times. I shrank beneath all the stares. "Sorry..."

The king leaned forward and glared at me. "You disapprove of my offer?"

Cayden stepped between us. "What would you have from my people?"

"I would have a shipment of twelve dozen sheep sent to my realm every week," the king demanded.

Cayden started back and his eyes widened. "So many? But the flocks of my own people would soon be depleted."

Cathal stood. "That is your problem to solve, dragon king, but I will allow you time to think over my proposal. In the meanwhile, you will be shown to-"

"A moment, Your Highness." Xander moved forward to stand shoulder-to-shoulder with Cayden. He nodded at the red dragon who smirked back. "Why do you invite a traitor to your court?"

The red dragon bowed to Xander. "I am merely a lamb lost without its shepherd and guided here by pity for the plight of the humans."

Xander's eyes narrowed. "There is not enough pity in the whole of the Bestia Draconis to find compassion for a fly."

The stranger straightened and chuckled. "Perhaps the dragon lord is blinded by his prejudice?"

"I am not blinded from the truth," Xander snapped.

Cathal raised one hand. "Whatever qualms you have among yourselves is of no concern to me. However-" he cast a warning glance at the red dragon and Xander, "-I will not tolerate fighting among my guests. If you wish to destroy one another do so over the ocean."

The red dragon bowed his head to the king. "I would rather keep peace in your territory, Your Highness. Besides-" his eyes darted to Xander, "-this dragon cannot fly."

Xander ground his teeth together. Spiros set a hand on his shoulder, and my dragon lord turned his tense face away from the red dragon.

Cathal looked to his right. A small contingent of the guards broke off and marched over to us. "Show them to their rooms." The guards bowed to their king and turned to us with a clack of their boots.

Our little group was marched out of the throne room and down the wide hall. Halfway down we took a left into a narrower hall that allowed me to sidle up to Xander. I leaned toward him. "You okay?" I whispered.

He stiffly nodded. "Yes."

"Want to talk about it?"

"No."

I frowned and straightened. "You're as moody as a brooding hen. What's wrong?"

Our entourage stopped in front of a few elegant wooden doors. One of them stepped out of the crowd and gestured to the entrances. "These will be your rooms while you are here. Don't wander the halls except to leave the royal residence."

"Thank you, captain," Cayden replied. The leader bowed and the guards marched off.

Xander looked to Spiros. "Watch Miriam. Cayden and I will make inquiries about the trouble here."

I crossed my arms over my chest and glared at him. "Have you forgotten that I beat you at the get-out-of-bed game? If there's trouble, I want to be there."

"That is why you must remain with Spiros, and I will have Cayden at my side. He will hold my promise to keep you safe until my strength returns," he insisted.

My eyes flickered to Spiros. "Why don't we all just go together instead of this splitting up-" I glanced back to Xander. He and Cayden were halfway down the hall. "Hey! Wait-" I rushed after them, but Spiros caught my shoulder. I spun around and glared at him. "Come on, Spiros, you know I'm right. We need to stick together."

He smiled and shook his head. "You have a gift for finding more trouble than Xander and I are able to manage. It would be best if you remained here."

I tapped my chin and rolled my eyes to the ceiling. "How about no?"

I turned on a dime and raced down the tiled corridor. My pounding feet were the only noise that followed me. I reached the intersection and glanced over my shoulder. The hall was empty. Spiros was gone.

I straightened and turned my head left and right. "Spiros? Spiros, you there?" No reply.

To make matters worse, I didn't see Cayden or Xander anywhere, either. There were a dozen different halls they could have followed.

My arms drooped and I glared at the many halls. "This is a fun house, but I'm not having much fun."

I decided sticking around wouldn't be much fun, either, so I made my way to the front doors. The bright sunlight of the fresh day greeted me like an old friend and welcomed me with warm, open arms.

I wandered forth into the wilds of the metropolis. My attire caught the attention of many of the sheep-attired locals. Many of the people I saw were women with their young children in tow.

It was a soothing sight, but all this walking was going to get me nowhere fast. I stepped toward my fellow wanderers, but they turned off into side streets or hurried past. Others, seeing my actions, gave me a wide berth so that I soon found myself alone in the middle of the streets.

After five terraces my feet complained about the hard ground. I found myself at a large square, one of many that dotted the terraces and chatted among themselves at the wells. Their children raced each other up and down the cobblestoned roads, or played a form of jacks with the bones of sheep.

I took a seat on a stone bench at the edge of one of the square and watched the serene pandemonium. A small group of young children kicked a rubber ball between themselves. One of them kicked a little too hard and the ball bounced over to me. I leaned down and caught the wayward toy in both hands. It was squishy and a little sticky in spots.

One of the children, a girl dressed in a short, silk-thin wool dress dyed red, hurried over to me. She stopped a yard short of the bench and glanced from the ball in my hands to my face.

I smiled and held out the ball. "It's a very pretty ball."

She returned the smile and took the ball. "Thank you. . ."

"What's it made out of?"

"Sheep bladder."

My smile froze on my face. I resisted the urge to run to the well to wash my hands. "That's neat. By the way, you didn't happen to see some tall men come by, did you? They wore funny clothing."

OCEANS BENEATH DRAGONS

She shook her head and scampered back to her friends. I sighed and gingerly wiped my hands on my jeans, but paused halfway through my chore. Movement out of the corner of my eye caught my attention, and I glanced to my left.

There, half hidden by the shadows of a narrow alley, stood the girl from the trees. Her full attention lay on me. I stood and took a step toward her. "Could you-" She beckoned to me with one hand and disappeared down the alley. "Hey! Wait!"

CHAPTER 18

I hurried to the mouth of the alley. The young woman was fifty yards ahead of me and gaining ground. I groaned. "Why does this always have to be so hard?"

I sprinted down the alley after the young woman. My mysterious guide led me up the many terraces to the top of the valley. We were on the opposite side of the city from the bay path. The trees were farther between, but far taller. Their branches created canopies that resembled the terraces in the valley behind me. Their branches were so thick that nothing grew beneath them save for knee-high grass.

I paused on the precipice of the forest. At my back lay civilization. Before me was a wide, well-trodden dirt path that led into the wilds of the unknown island. My guide was nowhere to be seen. Nothing stirred save when a breeze gently rocked the leaves.

I gingerly stepped into the shadows of the giant trees and looked around. "Hello?" My voice echoed down the path. I took a few more steps. "Are you-" A soft sound of feet hitting bare dirt came from behind me.

I spun around and found the young woman standing behind me on the path. She clasped her hands together in front of her and bowed to me. "It is a pleasure to meet you."

I glanced around us. There wasn't anywhere where she could have hidden. My eyes settled back on the young woman as she straightened. "Where'd you come from?"

A soft smile slipped onto her lips. "I am not allowed to tell you, but I can tell you where your friends have gone."

I perked up. "Two men?"

She nodded. "Yes. They went in there-" she nodded at the path behind me, "-in search of the Sacred Grove."

I arched an eyebrow. "The what?"

"The Sacred Grove is where all of the sheep are kept," she explained.

I half-turned to get a better look at the path. There wasn't any sign of an opening in the trees. I glanced to my right at the young woman. "I wouldn't be ruining your friendships if I asked you to show me the way, would I?"

Her bright smile faltered. She closed her eyes and shook her head. "I have no friends, only my-that is, my grandmother."

I smiled and jerked my head in the direction of the path. "Then we could both really use a friend right now, so how about we get acquainted while you show me the way to this grove place?"

Her chipper smile returned and she hurried to my side where she bowed her head again. "I promise to be a good friend."

I grinned and patted her shoulder. "You can start being a good friend by looking up and telling me your name."

She raised her head. "My name is Roisin. Roisin Brady."

I held out my hand. "Mine's Miriam Cait." She stared blankly at my hand until I grasped hers and clasped ours together in a hearty shake before I separated us. "So when'd you see those two guys come by here?" She raised her hand and gawked at her appendage. I arched an eyebrow and leaned toward her. "You okay?"

Roisin dropped her hand and stood at attention. "Y-yes. Only-well, save for my grandmother I have never touched another being."

"Seriously?"

She tilted her head to one side and studied me. "Should I not be serious?"

I waved off my comment. "Never mind. I'll just guess you're being serious, but I don't understand why you're not walking around the city with a parade of guys behind you. You're pretty cute, and they've got to love the blue eyes."

Roisin bit her lower lip and turned her face away from me. She drew her arms around herself and shook her head. "They prefer brown eyes."

I looped one of her arms threw mine and tugged her down the path. "Then you should get off this place and go find a nice guy who likes blue eyes."

She whipped her head up and her eyes widened. "Leave Ui Breasail?"

"Yeah. Maybe go to some place that's easier to pronounce."

A small giggle escaped her pressed lips. "Ui Breasail is not hard to pronounce."

"Have you ever met a foreigner who didn't have trouble pronouncing it?" I teased.

She shook her head. "Oh, no. Only the men are allowed to speak with foreigners, and only when they trade the wool."

I rolled my eyes. "Typical. So is that all they do?"

"The men also look after the sheep now that there are so few left," she told me. She looked ahead and pursed her lips. "They try to protect them, but they continue to disappear."

"In this Sacred Grove place?" I guessed.

Roisin nodded. "Yes. The Grove is the safest point on the island. It cannot be reached from the coast without first going through the city, and the trees provide cover should they need to be hidden from danger in the sky."

I rubbed my chin with my free hand. "Sounds like a tough mystery to crack. How far is this place?"

She looked ahead of us. The grass around us was now waist-deep and the thick canopy blocked most of the sun. "We should reach the Grove soon, but there are a great many dangers before us."

I glanced around at the calm woods and thick grass. "What kind of-"

"Look out!" Roisin dove at me and shoved me to the ground. The force of the blow slammed me into the hard dirt path.

I rolled over and glared at her. "What's the matter-" My eyes widened as a scythe-like blade swung over our heads like a diabolical pendulum of slicy death.

I found the thick wool rope that held the death machine and followed it up to the treetops where it disappeared into the canopy. "This way," Roisin instructed me. She crawled across the ground for ten feet and stood.

I was close behind and climbed to my feet before I turned back to the trap. The scythe now hung as innocent as an unused guillotine. I looked to Roisin and jerked my thumb at the mechanism. "How many more of those are there?"

She smiled. "Many more, but I know where they all are. If you will follow me the others will not be released."

"Gladly. . ." I mumbled as I let her lead me down the path.

We meandered left and right along the path, and sometimes completely off it to escape setting off more traps. I tilted my head back and inspected the branches above us. My keen sense of self-preservation spotted a few suspicious ropes masquerading as vines that dangled from the canopy.

"So why do you guys have so many traps this way?" I asked her.

"The traps are to protect the remaining sheep from theft," she told me.

I arched an eyebrow. "So they're being stolen?"

She pursed her lips. "I cannot say more."

"Not even between friends?" I persisted.

Roisin turned her face away from me and hung her head. "Please do not make me choose between our friendship and my people."

I looped my arm through one of hers and smiled at her downcast face. "Could you at least tell me what's so sacred about this place? You know, where it got its name?"

She raised her head and brightened her expression with a smile. "Of course. There is a pond in the middle which was once revered by my ancestors. A god was said to inhabit the waters and they prayed to him for strong lambs."

"So did the god move away or something?" I wondered.

She shook her head. "No, at least, I do not believe so. The island was struck by a terrible earthquake a thousand years ago. Much of the coastline was changed and the forests were toppled by a great wave. My ancestors sought the highest ground on the island and survived, but when they went to offer thanks to their god for their survival they found that the food was not accepted."

I blinked at her. "The food wasn't accepted?"

Roisin nodded. "Yes. They had always left an offering of sheep for their god, and the next day the meat would always be gone. Now it was not so. The food remained until they removed the meat themselves, and gradually my people stopped believing in the god." She turned her attention to the path ahead of us. "We are near the Sacred-"

A dark shadow flew down from the trees and landed ten feet ahead of us. Roisin and I jerked to a stop as the figure stood and revealed himself to be the red dragon from the palace. His large, red leathery wings were stretched out behind him like a silky fire.

He drew them into his back as he crossed one arm over his chest and bowed low to us. "Good day, my ladies. What brings two fine-looking women to the dark heart of the island?"

I stepped in front of Roisin and glared at him. "We could ask you the same question."

He straightened and revealed a sly, crooked smile. "I merely wished to see once again the face of the woman whom the fae have named Neito Vedesta."

"My name's Miriam," I insisted.

His smile widened. "You have many names, dear lady. Miriam. Maiden. Neito Vedesta." He tilted his head to one side and studied me. "Suta Varunanam."

I arched an eyebrow. "What's that supposed to mean?"

Roisin tugged on my arm and leaned toward me to whisper into my ear. "We must hurry."

He took a step toward us. "I cannot allow your passage, Miriam. Your presence may have a calming effect on the locals, and that would spoil my sincere wish to help them."

I snorted. "All you want to do is help yourself."

He grinned. "Such stunning introspection from a female who hardly knows what she is."

I stepped toward him and held out my fist. "I may not know what I am, but that won't stop me from trying to get past."

The dragon unfurled his red wings and blocked the wide path. "Then bring forth your wrath on me, Mare Fae, and we shall-" He whipped his head up and frowned.

Roisin and I followed his gaze. A shadow flew over us and landed on the path between us and the red dragon. I recognized the green wings and military attire of Spiros as he straightened and set his hand on the butt of his sword.

"I must ask that you duel with me," Spiros demanded.

The red dragon sneered at him. "So the false Grand Dragon Lord's puppet makes his appearance."

I put my hands on my hips and glared at him. "Where the hell have you been?"

Spiros turned his head to one side and glanced over his shoulder at me with a sly smile. "One step behind you, My Lady." He returned his attention to our foe. "The king has ordered us to lay aside our differences, but I assure you I will not lay aside my sword if my lady needs protecting."

The red dragon stepped backward into the deeper shadows of the trees. His red, narrowed eyes glowed in the darkness. "Savor this small, pointless victory, puppet. It may be your last."

"At least my strings are not so hidden, nor my allegiance," Spiros returned.

The red dragon snarled, but flapped his long wings. He flew into the canopy and disappeared. Soon we couldn't even hear the flap pf his wings.

Spiros relaxed and let drop his hand before he turned to me with a smile. "Do you ever tire of trouble, Miriam?"

I glared at him. "You were following me this whole time?"

His eyes twinkled. "My orders were to protect you, not to lead you to Xander." He glanced at Roisin. "Though it appears my efforts failed."

I looped my arm through one of hers and nodded. "You bet it did. Come on, Roisin, let's go find the guys."

"But I-" I tugged her along with me past Spiros and down the path. Spiros followed close behind us.

We'd only gone fifty yards when we heard noises ahead of us.

"We need no help from your kind!" The loud, masculine voice echoed down the path and caused my guide to jerk to a stop.

"We only wish to avert war," Cayden's voice replied.

Roisin slunk behind me and grasp my shoulders. "I-I should not be here. . ." she whispered.

I looked over my shoulder at her and smiled. "Come on, these are your people, right?"

She shook her head and stepped back away from me. "I am sorry, but I cannot go any farther with you." She spun around and raced past Spiros.

He caught her arm and stopped her retreat before he gazed into her eyes. "You cannot hide what you are forever."

Roisin's eyes widened. She yanked herself from his grasp and sprinted down the path. Soon she was gone.

I glared at Spiros. "Why'd you have to scare her like that?"

"Attention, men!" the male voice barked.

Spiros frowned and rushed forward. I stretched out my hand and stumbled after him. "Hey! Wait for me!"

I was a dozen yards behind him when the path climbed a short hill and opened. Before me was spread a magnificent meadow of thick, green grass. Short, rolling hills slid up to the dense forest that surrounded all sides of the grassy field. A large pond lapped gently at its sandy shores to my left, and at the edge of the water was a flock of some three hundred white-puffed sheep.

Among the grass was also a contingent of sheep-skulled guards, and they had Xander and Cayden surrounded.

CHAPTER 19

Spiros slowed his pace and strode down the hill toward them. I hurried up to his side. We were just in time to hear the more nuanced parts of the conversation.

"We would rather die than be given your assistance!" one of the skull-attired gentleman growled. He stood in the circle of armed men and glared at Cayden and Xander.

Cayden stepped forward. "But we-" The soldiers stepped closer to them and drew their swords.

Xander set his hand on Cayden's shoulder and swept his gaze over the tense crowd. "We only request an explanation for your troubles. That is all."

"That's too much!" the leader snapped.

By now Spiros and I stood thirty feet off. The captain had his hand on the butt of his sword. Xander's eyes flickered to us, and he gently shook his head.

I narrowed my eyes, rolled up my sleeves and marched up to the line of solders that surrounded my dragon lord and his companion. "A lady is coming through!" I yelled.

The men, being trained far longer in etiquette than military commands, hurriedly parted, and I stomped into the circle. Both the leader and Xander glared at me. I crossed my arms over my chest and glared back. "What the hell's going on?"

Xander stepped toward me. "Miriam, please-" I held up my hand.

"Oh no, no 'Miriam, please go away.' You're in my problems then I'm in your problems, and this-" I pointed at the leader and his men, "-this is a lot of problems."

The leader narrowed his eyes at me. "We are not the ones who are trespassing." His eyes flickered to Xander and he pursed his lips. "The offense is worse for those who are not human."

"So how do I fit into this trespassing rules?" I challenged him.

The man sneered at me and spat on the ground. "Anyone who willingly cavorts with dragons is no human to us."

I put my hands on my hips and narrowed my eyes. "So you're going to what? Hit an unarmed girl?" The men around me glanced at each other. Some shifted uneasily from foot to foot.

The leader straightened and lifted his chin in the air. "We do not harm women, even those who forsake their own kind."

"Then how about we drop all this trespass stuff and you just tell us what's wrong," I suggested.

He frowned at me. "Our problems are our own. Do not interfere."

I opened my mouth, but Xander set a heavy hand on my shoulder. I whipped my head around, but the dark look in his green eyes told me a snarky reply wouldn't be appreciated.

Xander drew me back behind him so he was between the leader and me. "We apologize for the trespass, and swear it will not happen again."

The human sneered at him and nodded at the open path behind us. "Then leave, but be warned I will report this blasphemy to King Cathal and he will decide for himself what is to be done with you lot."

Xander bowed his head. "We will abide by his verdict."

Xander turned me around and the men grudgingly parted to allow the three of us to exit from the uncomfortable circle. Spiros attached himself to our little group, and together the four of us returned to the path.

We had gone fifty feet when I tried to shrug off Xander's stubborn hand. The hand stuck to my shoulder. "I'm not going to wander off."

Xander looked ahead, but spoke to Spiros who was behind us with Cayden. "Have they followed us?"

Spiros nodded his head. "Yes, but at a great distance."

"Then it cannot be helped." Xander stopped and turned to face our group. My shoulder was released along with my scolding. "You should have remained in the palace."

I frowned. "We're in this together, remember?"

"I do not wish for you to step into trouble of my making," he insisted.

I snorted. "You're starting to sound like those guys back there. Do you really think them telling us to shove off is going to help them solve their problem?" Xander pursed his lips. I leaned toward him and raised an eyebrow. "Well?"

My dragon lord sighed and ran a hand through his short hair. "No, and unfortunately it will not help us, either."

Cayden closed his eyes and shook his head. "I do not wish to start a war between our people, but I cannot see any way to free ourselves from that fate."

"There is another matter that may need our attention, Xander," Spiros spoke up.

Xander arched an eyebrow. "What is that?"

"The Bestia Draconis sought to stop Miriam and me from reaching the meadow," he explained.

I looked around at the dragon men. "And speaking of that, does anybody happen to know what Suta Vacuum means?"

"Suta Varunanam," Spiros corrected me.

I jerked my thumb at him. "What he said."

Xander whipped his head to me and narrowed his eyes. His expression was tense and his words came out as a sharp demand. "Where did you hear those words?"

"That red dragon guy said that to me," I revealed. Xander stared straight ahead and pursed his lips. My eyebrows crashed down. "So what's it mean?"

He shook himself from his thoughts looked back to me. "The words mean the Bestia Draconis have learned of your fae lineage, and they wish for us to know they have such knowledge."

"But what does it mean?" I insisted.

"The title is in the ancient language of my dragon ancestors and roughly translates to 'Child of Varuna,'" he explained.

I blinked at him. "And that means?"

"A child of water, as you are a child of Mare Fae."

I rolled my eyes. "Why didn't he just say that?"

"The ancient tongue of dragons has long been abandoned, and only those of noble lineage bother to learn its intricacies. Thus he used the old to relay the message directly to me," he surmised.

"Knowing what they know, do you believe they may harm Miriam?" Cayden wondered.

Xander pursed his lips and shook his head. "I do not know. The Mare Fae are a rare breed, and one born with a human parent is even less common. Whatever plans they may have, we will have to meet them as they come without any foreknowledge."

I raised my hand. "Hello? I'm still standing here with you guys. And speaking of that, too-" I looked to Xander. "How'd you guys know how to get to the Sacred Grove?"

Xander arched an eyebrow. "How did you come to learn its name?"

I jerked my thumb over my shoulder in the direction of the city. "A girl named Roisin told me. She also led me here. Well, until someone-" I glanced at Spiros with narrowed eyes, "-scared her off."

He shook his head. "It was not I who frightened her. She wished to avoid the humans."

I snorted. "Why'd she want to avoid humans when she is one?"

"Do you believe she would help us learn of the troubles here?" Xander asked me.

I shrugged. "Maybe. She helped me already."

Xander looked to Spiros. "Can you track where she went?"

The experienced captain nodded. "Yes, but without prior knowledge of the island and with your wings as they are we will be forced to track on foot."

My dragon lord gave a nod. "Then we must do so. Lead on."

CHAPTER 20

We traveled down the path and back to the city. Spiros, who was in the lead, paused at the entrance to the path and stooped. He brushed his fingers against the hard-packed dirt before he glanced to our left. "The trail leads along the edges of the city, but we may lose her in the trees."

I raised an eyebrow. "Why?"

He stood. "She is very adept at flitting through the trees."

"So she's part monkey?" I guessed. I received three blank starts for that one. "You know, the tree-swinging animal?" Cayden shook his head. My shoulders slumped. "Never mind."

"Let us hurry or we will lose what little trail she will leave behind," Xander insisted.

Our little group skirted the edge of the uppermost tier of the city until we reached a small, barely-noticeable path into the trees. Spiros guided us onto the path and into the quiet forest. The manicured woods fell away and before us was a wilderness of natural beauty. Bushes hugged the trunks of trees and thick vines climbed up to the branches and spread themselves across the wide, dense canopy. The trail became littered with rocks that tripped me at every turn, and the flat ground transformed into a bumpy path of potholes and small hills. It was like being home on a good stretch of road.

We walked for a mile before the path followed a short, steep hill and opened into a small clearing. A hut made of notched trees with a foundation of stones stood in the center of the clearing. To our right was a small, hoed plot with vegetables and a few fruit trees beside that. On our left the trees disappeared and presented us with a beautiful view of the rugged coastline and the wide, endless ocean.

Our presence didn't go unnoticed. The heavy door of the hut swung open, and in the doorway stood a short, plump old woman. Her gray hair and wrinkled face denoted her seventy odd years of life. She wore a long gray dress over her round form, and an apron covered her front. Her gray hair was pulled back in a single braid that trailed behind her down to her hips. In her hand was a grenade.

I did a double-take on that assessment. The grenade was ovular like the man-made death machine, but the sides were smooth and the body squished in her hand. The unmistakable odor of Dragon's Bane wafted over to us.

"What's wanted?" she snarled.

Xander held up his hands in front of him and stepped to the front of our group. "We wish to speak with the girl who calls herself Roisin."

The woman narrowed her eyes. "Why?"

Xander gestured to me. "She assisted my Maiden a short while ago. We are in desperate need of her help once again."

The old woman took a step toward us and drew back her hand that held the grenade. "All you dragon folk are liars. Why should I entrust you with my granddaughter?"

I raised my hand. "I'm not a dragon."

Her eyes fell on me and she turned up her nose. "No, but you're not human, either, your eyes tell me as much, and you're still following him around. That counts against you."

"We only wish to help those on this island," Cayden insisted.

She raised an eyebrow. "Help how?"

Xander shook his head. "We do not know until we have learned more about the troubles on the island."

Our erstwhile hostess frowned and tilted her head a little to her right. "Roisin!"

A shadow stepped out from the far corner of the house and slunk to the front. Roisin stepped out into the sunlight. Her head was bowed and her eyes were on the ground. "Y-yes, Grandmother?"

The old woman jerked her head towards us. "Did you help them?"

Roisin cringed, but nodded. "Yes, Grandmother."

"Why?"

Roisin lifted her head an inch and glanced at me. Her tense face softened. "I thought I might help her."

"But why?" her grandmother persisted.

Roisin flinched. "So we could be friends."

Her grandmother pursed her lips. "You've caused a mess of-"

"Xander, the soldiers," Spiros spoke up.

Xander and Spiros swung around, and Cayden and I followed suit. From the dense forest came a small contingency of skull-wearing men. They encircled our small group and pointed the sharp tops of their long halberds at us.

The last person to enter the clearing was the ram-headed king himself, Cathal. At his hip was his ram-skull, and in his own hand was a towering halberd made of polished steel-like metal. His lips were pressed so tightly together they were white. He marched up to us and stopped on the outskirts of our entrapment. "I have been made aware of your transgression in the Sacred Grove, and command that you leave my island at once."

Cayden stepped up to the human wall of our prison. "But Your Highness, you must understand my people cannot continue to suffer. If you would only allow us to help you."

The king frowned. "You know how you may assist us, and yet you refused."

"Let us assist you here!" Cayden pleaded.

King Cathal shook his head. "No words of yours can convince me you are not here for other purposes. Not when you have purposefully traveled to this small clearing." He stepped aside and nodded down the path to his right. "Men, escort them to the dock." A great din arose from my companions and the metal halberds as they created a wall to shove us forward.

"Wait!" The soft, sharp voice cut through the protests and clanks of metal. Everyone turned to the source of the cry, Roisin. She clasped her hands together in front of her and wrung them in the direction of the king. "Please do not take them! Please!"

Cathal's eyes flickered to the young woman's grandmother. "What is the meaning of this, Mac Bradaigh?" I furrowed my brow. That name. . .

The old woman studied her granddaughter with pursed lips. "What's come over you?"

Roisin hurried over to her grandmother and clasped the old woman's hands before she looked into her eyes. "Please let them stay. I have waited so long for one who was like me, and. . .and now that I have found her-" she hung her head and fought back tears, "-please, Grandmother. Please let them stay."

Her grandmother shook her head. "They can't stay, and they shouldn't."

Cathal took that as his signal. "Men!"

The men shoved their metal spears against us and herded us toward the forest. The protests were deafening.

"Let us help you!" cried Cayden.

"Please, Grandmother!" Roisin pleaded.

"Dragons can't be trusted," Mac Bradaigh insisted.

Dragon. Mac Bradaigh. That's when the memory hit me. I twisted my head around to face the old woman. "Dreail!"

Her eyes widened and her mouth dropped open. "What was that?"

I couldn't answer. One of our escort gave me a particularly hard nudge down the path. I glared at him. "Watch it!"

Mac Bradaigh stumbled toward us. "Stop!"

Our march stopped and the king turned to her with a frown. "What is the matter?"

Mac Bradaigh ignored him and hurried up to me. She searched my face. "Where'd you hear that name?"

"An old sea dragon has it, and he has yours, too," I told her.

She scoffed. "He's probably forgotten about me by now."

I shook my head. "Nope. He remembers you as a pretty feisty girl, and he wants to see you and your family."

"Then why doesn't he get out his wings and come see me?" she snapped. I opened my mouth, but the words caught in my throat. She sniffed at me. "I thought so. He doesn't want to see me or any of my family."

"Age has found him, and his wings will no longer hold him," Xander spoke up.

She arched an eyebrow. The corners of her lips twitched up. "So he's as shriveled as I am, is he?"

Xander smiled and bowed his head. "He is."

"I'd say a little more shrively," I chimed in.

King Cathal stepped up to her side and caught her gaze. "These trespassers cannot remain. They know too much."

I nodded at Mac Bradaigh. "If you're trying to keep us from knowing she's the one building your Dragon Bane balls, you're a little late. Dreail told us that already."

The king started back before he narrowed his eyes. "Then you have spoken too much about what you know. We cannot allow you to leave here alive."

Mac Bradaigh spun around to face him and put her hands on her wide hips. "You're not going to touch a hair on any of their heads."

Cathal shook his head. "We cannot allow-"

"I heard you before, but if you had half your mind working you'd know they weren't asking me about that," she scolded him.

The king frowned. "It must be some trick of theirs-"

"It is no trick, Your Highness," Xander spoke up among our cramped group. "We only wish to help you so no people will suffer."

Cathal pursed his lips. Mac Bradaigh rolled her eyes. "Just let them go, Colin. No one's believing you." The men around us shifted from one foot to another, glanced at each other with wide grins, and some of them even snickered.

The king's face reddened and he glared at the soldiers. "At attention!" The men stiffened and faced straight ahead. Cathal's narrowed eyes flickered to Mac Bradaigh and he pursed his lips so tightly we barely heard the next command. "Release them."

The men raised their halberds against their sides and stepped backward. Cayden stepped to the front of our group between Cathal and us, and bowed to the king. "Thank you for your kindness, Your Highness."

He sneered at Cayden. "It is only by the grace of Mac Bradaigh that you are allowed to live."

"And don't be forgetting about it too soon," she spoke up.

Cayden smiled at her and bowed his head. "I see now why you have held Dreail's attention for so long. You are an admirable woman."

Mac Bradaigh frowned, but her back straightened and she puffed out her chest a little. "I don't know about that, and I don't care a lick about that old fool, but if you can help with this sheep problem then you're worth having around for a little while longer."

"What is the problem?" Xander spoke up.

Cathal pursed his lips. Mac Bradaigh glared at him. "Go on! Tell them!"

He half-turned away from us and toward the path. "It would be easier to show you. Follow me." He and his men marched down the path. Cayden, Spiros and Xander followed.

I hesitated and glanced over my shoulder. Mac Bradaigh turned to Roisin and jerked her head toward our group. "Go on. Go with them."

Roisin's eyes widened. "Me? But why?"

Mac Bradaigh grinned. "Because there's no man on the island as strong as you, and this is as good a time as ever to be showing all them what you're made of."

Her granddaughter's face was brightened with a smile. Roisin threw herself onto Mac Bradaigh and gave her a big hug before she pulled them arm's length apart. "Thank you."

Mac Bradaigh wrinkled her nose, but her eyes twinkled. "Bah. Now off you go, and don't be afraid to show yourself off."

Roisin nodded and rushed over to me. She grabbed my hand and smiled at me. "I am ready, friend."

I returned the smile. "Good. I'd hate to leave a friend behind. Now let's get going before we're left behind."

CHAPTER 21

We hurried down the trail and caught up to the tail. Xander and the others were buried in the ranks of soldiers near Cathal.

I kept us back and looked Roisin over. "So I'm guessing your grandma's the person who raised you."

Roisin was all smiles as she nodded. "Yes."

"She seems like a pretty tough customer." Roisin gave me a blank look. I sighed. "I mean she looks pretty stern."

My new friend nodded. "She is, but she is very fair. Many from the city come to her for judgment with their problems."

I arched an eyebrow and studied her. "So how come you don't speak like her?"

Roisin blushed and looked away. "I speak as the city-dwellers speak so I might communicate easily with them."

"But they didn't want to talk to you," I guessed.

Her shoulders fell and she shook her head. "No, they did not."

"Why?"

Roisin bit her lower lip. "I would rather not say."

I gave her a nudge and a smile. "What's a little secret between-"

"What a pleasure to meet such beautiful ladies once more." Roisin and I started forward when the red dragon made his appearance from behind us. He split us in two with his arrival and held his customary smirk on his lips as he looked first from Roisin then to me. "Have I startled you?"

I glared at him. "No, we just don't like the stench of asshole."

His smirk never faltered. "I must remember to change my scent with perfume. You both, however-" he leaned toward me and sniffed the air as his eyes flickered to Roisin, "-you hold some rather unique smells." He grasped my arm with his cold, clammy hand. "What secrets does your-"

His sick romancing was interrupted when a hand grabbed the red dragon from behind and yanked him backward. The dragon stumbled a few yards before he regained his balance and glared at the interloper, Spiros. The captain of the Alexandrian guard pressed his lips together and whistled a high-pitched tune.

I glared at my old friend. "You were stalking us again, weren't you?"

He kept his narrow-eyed gaze on the red dragon as he spoke. "I was merely watching you."

Things got interesting when Xander pushed through the crowd of soldiers with Cayden and Cathal close at his heels. The whole company stopped as my dragon lord faced off against our red-winged foe. "What is the matter?"

Spiros nodded at the dragon. "He meant to interfere with Miriam."

The red dragon scoffed. "I meant no such thing. I was merely chatting with the young women."

I snorted. "Maybe small talk for a viper."

Cathal glared at him. "I ordered you not to bring your differences to my island."

The red dragon bowed to him. "My apologies if my sign of friendship was taken as an assault on the beautiful Maiden. I meant no disrespect."

"Then why did you follow us so far in secret?" Spiros challenged him.

Our foe smiled and shook his head. "I cannot imagine to what you refer, but seeing as I am not welcomed here I will take my leave." He bowed to King Cathal. "If you will excuse me, Your Highness."

He turned and walked away. Xander turned to the king. "I would advise you to keep careful watch of that dragon, Your Highness."

The king smirked. "None of my guests are ever alone on my island. He will be watched."

Our large group continued on to the open meadow. We were greeted by the same friendly group who had threatened our lives before. The leader marched up to Cathal and saluted before he glared at us. "All is well here, My King."

"That is well, Captain Garda, but did the reports sent to me this morning not say others had disappeared?" Cathal wondered. The man glanced past his king and at us. Cathal half-turned and followed his gaze to our group. "They have convinced me of their sincerity, and shall assist in find the culprit who steals our sheep. Whatever you have to say to me may be said in their presence."

Garda pursed his lips, but returned his attention to Cathal. "The reports are accurate, My King. Another five have vanished."

"What exactly happens, Your Highness?" Cayden spoke up.

Cathal frowned. "Four months ago our sheep began to disappear. The quantity was not great, never more than three, but they were taken at least every other night. I have kept guards around the Sacred Grove, but though they are diligence and observant they have seen nothing of the thieves."

I wandered away from the group and mingled among the grazing sheep. They gave the pool of water a wide berth and kept mostly to the perimeter of the meadow. Along the side opposite the path entrance stretched a wooden watering trough. The fresh timbers and glistening nails told me it was new.

I looked over my shoulder at the others and nodded at the trough. "Why's that here?"

Garda followed my nod and pursed his lips. "The sheep have often refused to drink from the pond since the others began to disappear."

I pointed at the pond. "That's the one with the god, right?"

Xander arched an eyebrow and looked to the king. "What god is this?"

Cathal scoffed. "It is nothing more than legend. An old tale to amuse our children."

Roisin stepped forward and swept her gaze over the group. "But the tales are true. A god was once there."

Cathal looked to her and his eyebrows crashed down. "Only a fool would believe a god resided in a pond when all wise men know there are no gods."

I walked over and put my hand on her shoulder before I glared at Cathal. "Then I guess I'm a fool because I believe in gods, and I believe there was one in that pond, because you know what-"

"Miriam," Xander spoke up.

I whipped my head to him. "What?"

He closed his eyes and shook his head before he turned his attention to Cathal. "Perhaps what is needed is fewer men."

Cathal arched an eyebrow. "Why is that?"

Xander nodded at the men that surrounded the meadow. "The thieves are bold, but they may be more bold were no one to be seen."

The king furrowed his brow. "Your idea has a great flaw. How is anyone to stop them if no one is there?"

The sun caught on the polished bones of the skull. That's when the crazy idea hit me.

"We could get somebody kidnapped with the sheep," I suggested. All eyes turned on me, and many had questioning glances. I shrugged. "Why not?"

King Cathal arched an eyebrow. "What do you mean?"

I nodded at the skull helmet that lay against his hip. "Somebody could dress up as a sheep and when the thieves come to steal them they could give a shout or something."

The king folded his arms and slowly nodded. "Your idea has merit. My men will try it this very night."

"And I will volunteer myself as the lamb to slaughter," Xander offered.

"As will I," Spiros spoke up.

"It's my idea, so I get to do it," I insisted. I crossed my arms and looked the men up and down. "Besides, you guys are a little big for sheep."

Xander shook his head. "I will not allow you to-" I stomped my foot against the ground and put my hand on my hip.

"You can't protect me forever, and even if you could I don't think I'd want you to," I argued.

He pursed his lips. "What do you mean?"

I stepped forward and grasped his hands before I looked him in the eyes. "I love your chivalry, and you're so cute when you're playing the hero and saving my life all the time, but I want to be a part of this. I want to be a part of *your life*, and I can't do it from the sidelines."

He blinked at me. "The 'sidelines?'"

I rolled my eyes. "I can't do it from the rear, okay? I'll just keep stepping on your heels, so how about we do this protecting thing together, side-by-side?"

A small, crooked smile slipped onto his lips. "You have the face of an angelic being and the wisdom of a seer."

"And I'm as stubborn as a mule and won't take 'no' for an answer," I quipped.

Xander turned to Cathal. "My Maiden will be among your sheep and call out if something is amiss while we hide ourselves at a distance. Will that be satisfactory to you?"

Cathal pursed his lips. "One sentinel will hardly work to catch these cunning thieves. Allow one of my men to-"

"I will be a sheep," Roisin spoke up.

The king turned to her and frowned. "You are hardly a replacement for any of my men."

I marched to Roisin's side and draped my arm over her shoulders before I glared at Cathal. "I'm not taking anybody else with me. Besides, I don't think Mac Bradaigh would like it if you didn't let her help out. That's why she's here, remember?"

Cathal frowned. "Very well, but I take no responsibility toward her." His eyes flickered to Xander and Cayden. "We will set the women out in the field and hide ourselves an hour before dark."

Cayden bowed his head. "We look forward to assisting you, Your Highness."

Cathal marched around us with his men and left the field. Xander came up to stand beside me. His face was tense as he studied mine. "Are you sure you wish to perform this risky task?"

I jerked my thumb at the pond and winked at him. "If I have any trouble I'll just use a little bit of water to help me."

His eyes drilled into mine. "I feel your motive is not as altruistic as you wish it to appear."

I frowned. "What's that supposed to mean?"

"That you are hiding your true intention in volunteering," he returned.

I pursed my lips and looked past him at the pond. "Well, let's just say there's a legend about a water god that I'd like to see for myself."

He nodded, and looked past me at Roisin. "Do you also wish to go through with this task?"

She nodded. "Yes. I wish to prove myself to everyone, and to my grandmother."

I rubbed my hands together. "Now all we need to do is wait."

CHAPTER 22

The rest of the day passed without incident, and an hour before sunset all the parties gathered in the field. Cathal brought with him two sheep skins complete with attached heads and tails. One of his guards also held a wooden box.

I nodded at the box. "What's in there?"

Cathal removed the lid and drew out a hoof with straps attached to either side of the top. "You will need to use these to hide your footprints."

I took the hoof and cringed. "What if I just crawl on my hands and knees?"

"If you disagree with my suggestion one of my men will be glad to take your place," he warned me.

I whipped my head up and slapped on a tense smile on my lips. "It's fine. I can work with this."

Cathal moved on and his guard handed me the other three hooves. Roisin slipped up beside me and smiled. Her arms were full of the sheep skin with the hooves atop it. "At least with two of us we are more likely to be kidnapped."

My face drooped. "Let's hope it doesn't get that far."

Xander helped me on with my costume and Spiros assisted Roisin. Soon we were two more sheep among the grass. I turned toward the pond, but Xander grasped my upper arms and pecked a kiss on my lips. "Whatever may come, please return to me."

I smiled and nodded. The action made my sheep head bob. "Always."

He and the others hid themselves among the trees some fifty yards from the meadow. The shadows were long as Roisin and I trudged down the slope to the pond. A few of the sheep lifted their heads and stared at us, but soon returned to their grazing.

I stopped at the water's edge and gazed at my reflection in the clear, still water. The lamb head stared back at me, and beneath the head and wool was my small eyes. The hooves were strapped to my knees and hands, and their hard surfaces dug into my bones.

I shifted uneasily as Roisin came up beside me. "These hooves are killing me. What about you?" The sheep dipped down and took a drink from the pond. "Maybe we should have asked for some padding."

The sheep raised her head and stared at me. "Baa."

I sheepishly grinned. "Sorry. Honest mistake."

"Are you well?" Roisin asked me as she trotted up to my other side.

I sighed and shook my skull. "I hope these thieves are as stupid as me."

She chuckled. "You are not foolish. I think you are very brave to offer to help my people."

I lifted my head and looked out across the pond. "Yeah, well, I'm kind of hoping maybe that story about the god might be true."

Roisin tilted her head to one side and blinked at me. "Why?"

I shook my head. "No reason. Anyway, let's get sheeping."

We wandered around the edge of the pond and up the hill. The sun set amid the throbbing pain of my poor knees and hands. Darkness enveloped us, but not the sheep. They migrated to the top of the hill and lay themselves down around the new trough. The sky above us was a clear screen of twinkling stars. The picture of the meadow was one of serenity.

I tripped over a small rock and stumbled up to the edge of the pond. "God damn-" Movement. A ripple flow out from the center of the otherwise still pond.

I stretched my neck and squinted. The rings of the ripple gently lapped against the edges of the round pond. The disturbance vanished, but my unease didn't.

I looked over my shoulder. Roisin was five yards behind me. "Psst."

Roisin lifted her head from the grass. "What-"

"Over here!" I whispered.

A soft gurgling noise caught my attention and I glanced back at the pond. My weak eyes detected a large dark shadow just beneath the surface of the water. The figure was shaped like a person, but darted through the water like a fish. They circled the center of the pond, but never surfaced.

OCEANS BENEATH DRAGONS

Roisin hurried to my side and gasped as she beheld what I saw. I inched one of my hoofed hands toward the water and tried to relax my tense body. I whetted my lips for a nice, loud cry of alarm. The shadow darted up to the edge of the water and raised their head above the shallow surface.

This strange shadow was a young man of sixteen. His skin was pale and his soft features reminded me of the round rocks smoothed over by countless years of waves. He wore his bluish hair short, but some strands fell close to his eyes. He was dressed in a simple pair of shorts made from long, short strips of seaweed, and around his neck was a necklace of pearls. A devilish smile danced across his lips.

He also had blue eyes. Shockingly bright blue eyes. They were so bright they glowed in the still darkness. I was trapped by those blue eyes, glued to the spot as he reached out and grabbed one of my front 'legs.' He yanked me forward and dragged me into the water.

The cold chill of the pond woke me from my stupor. I thrashed and yanked on my arm, but his grip was as strong as any dragon. He dragged me deeper into the abyss of water, so deep that I wondered if we weren't in a lake rather than a pond. We sped through the water at a speed great enough to force my hair and wool backward. The fresh-water of the pond was replaced by the salty flavor of the open ocean. There must have been a hidden entrance in the pond to the open seas.

More pale young men appeared from the depths of the water, three in total. They were close in appearance except for the lack of a pearl necklace. One of the others had a hold of Roisin. She didn't struggle like me. I glimpsed her face beneath her disguise and her expression was blank.

The young merman who was without a sheep floated up to my captor. "What is wrong with the sheep?"

My captor tugged me deeper into the dark depths and shook his head. "I do not know. The spell seems to have worn from her mind."

The sheep-less merman floated up to my face. His eyes glowed as the other one had, but I didn't feel the soothing effects as before.

Instead I reached out and slapped him. My movements were slow, but I used my water magic to extend my reach and make it faster. He didn't have time to dodge before I got him in the cheek.

The merman flew back and grabbed his red cheek. His eyes no longer glowed, but they were wide and unblinking. "The sheep slapped me!"

My captor leaned his head back and laughed. "The sheep kicked you, you-" I socked him in the chin with my extended water fist. He released me and flew back to join his companion. "The sheep struck me!"

I kicked over to Roisin. Her captor, fearing the mad sheep, swam away. I grabbed one of Roisin's arms and slapped her in the face. She started back and the blank expression fled from her face. Her eyes swept over the darkness and the pale young men who gawked at these strange sheep.

The sight of the men made Roisin start back. Her disguise flew off in an eruption of leathery wings as the symbols of a dragon lineage burst from her back. I gasped. Our kidnappers did more than that.

"Demon sheep!" one of them shouted. They sped off in all directions and disappeared into the darkness.

OCEANS BENEATH DRAGONS

They were gone, but not our problems. My inadvertent gasp meant the air in my lungs was expelled into the endless salt waters. I took in a mouthful of water before I slapped my hands over my mouth. My lungs burned for oxygen. I couldn't hold back the instinct to breath. My hands burned with a bright blue light as my mind panicked. I unwillingly took a deep breath.

And found I could breathe. I started back, and in doing so separated my hands from my face. The precious oxygen disappeared. I slapped a hand over my mouth. The sweet air returned.

Roisin wasn't so fortunate. She thrashed and twisted in the water. Her cheeks were puckered as she fought against the urge to suck in air that wasn't there. I stretched out my free hand toward her. My dragon came forth, but in a more tendril-like form. He wrapped around her and pinned her thrashing arms to her side. She gasped and all her precious air escaped.

I swam over to her and pressed my air-providing hand over her mouth. She took in a deep breath. Her wild eyes calmed, but they were wide when she looked to me.

I sheepishly smiled at her, but the effort forced some air out of my mouth. Small bubbles slipped between us and floated upward.

My dragon that was wrapped around Roisin slithered off her and wrapped itself around my head. I floated backward and waved my arms around to bat it off, but the dragon formed itself into an impenetrable bubble.

"Get off me!" I shouted.

I paused and blinked. The bubble around my head not only held oxygen, but allowed my voice to carry beyond its borders and into the water. I could breathe and talk underwater. I swept my eyes around the bubble and whistled. "Not bad, Miriam. Not too bad."

I had one last loose end to deal with. I created another dragon that swam over to Roisin and wrapped around her head. She started back and tried to swim away, but the water creature held tight to her noggin.

"He's not going to hurt you," I told her.

Roisin stopped and turned her head left and right. The bubble turned with her. She tapped the bubble. Her finger made an impression that disappeared when she released pressure.

Roisin tilted her head to one side and studied me. "What are you?" she whispered.

I looked past her at the leathery wings that floated behind her. "I'd kind of like an explanation, too."

She winced and averted her eyes. "I-I did wish to tell you, but Mother ordered that I not tell any outsiders of my half-heritage."

"You mean Grandmother?" I corrected her.

She shook her head. "No. The woman whom others call Mac Bradaigh is my mother. As a half-dragon I age much slower than she, and so to strangers I am her granddaughter."

I nodded. "Makes sense. Mostly."

She studied me. "But what of you? How can you control the waters?"

I shrugged. "I'm just your normal, every-day half-water fae."

She blinked at me. "Only half? Are fae very powerful?"

I turned away and studied the darkness around us. "Maybe we should save the fae discussion for another day.

OCEANS BENEATH DRAGONS

You're scaring away our kidnappers means we don't have a way to get back, wherever back is."

She cringed. "I am sorry. I was so frightened that I had not time to think."

I floated to her side and looked around us. "That's all right. I would've gotten my wings out, too, if I had them." The dark waters pressed against us. I couldn't see any sign that would tell us which way was the surface and which was the deeper depths. "I hate to say this, but don't really know how we're going to get back to the pond."

Roisin blinked and pointed at her air bubble. "But you are able to give us breath here. Can you not draw us back?"

I shook my head. "I don't really have that much of a handle on this whole fae power thing, so that would be a 'no.'"

My friend bit her lip and swept her eyes over the darkness. "Then we may never find our way to the grove?"

I slipped my hand through hers and smiled. "We won't know until we try. Just follow me and keep your eyes peeled for some light."

Roisin started back. "But I do not wish to peel my eyes."

I snorted and gave her a gentle tug. "It's only a figure of speech. Just look around and see if you can find a way out of here, or maybe see some of those fishy guys that dragged us down here."

She nodded. "I will try."

CHAPTER 23

We floated through the dark, wet abyss along a path that was more hope than knowledge. The world was water born from shadow.

I glanced from my left to my right. Only a few loose air bubbles told me which ways were up and down. "Damn. . ."

Roisin clutched onto me with trembling hands as we floated through the abyss. "I-I c-cannot see anything."

I furrowed my brow as I looked at her. "Are you cold?"

She nodded. "Yes. C-can you n-not feel it?"

I shook my head and looked ahead. "No." I could feel it through Roisin's shirt. She had goosebumps on her arms.

I pursed my lips as I studied the eternal darkness. Maybe there were other water fae out there we could get a hold of, but how to call for help?

Call. I frowned. Abha had mentioned something about the Call, and that old man, too. I stopped and looked around.

"Is something the matter?" Roisin asked me.

I shook my head as I swept my eyes over the darkness. "No, but maybe. . ." I closed my eyes and listened.

The water was as silent as the grave, or was it? Every pond and stream had a current, and the ocean was just a larger version of those. I focused all my attention on my clothes and skin.

There. A slight touch of current brushed past me. It was the way we headed and pushed at our backs as though urging us gently along.

Something traveled along the currents, something I could barely hear. It was a soft melody, like someone whistling far away. I strained to hear the music. My lips pressed together as I sought to mimic the sound.

"Hmmhmm. Hmmhmm," I hummed. It was like a lullaby that cradled the deep. I only caught a bit of the music, but it was enough.

"What is that tune?" Roisin asked me.

I opened my eyes and grinned. "I think it might be our ticket out of here." I let go of her and swam a little ahead. The current brushed past me and into the depths of the ocean. I took a deep breath and cupped my hands over my mouth. "Hmmhmm! Hmmhmm!"

My voice echoed deep into the darkness. I waited. Roisin came up beside me and looked where I looked. There was only shadow.

Then she came. She started as a speck of light in the dark, but the closer she came the clearer became her form. She was a young woman of about twenty, or appeared to be. I admired her beautiful long blond hair that floated around her like a halo. Her attire kept with the moss-attire like the young men, but her breasts were covered, as well. A pearl necklace adorned her neck.

At her side was the young man with the same necklace. He hung back and hung his head. If there'd been ground beneath us he would have kicked at the dirt.

The young swam up to us as swift and clean as any dolphin. She looked from one of us to the other with wide eyes. "You are alive?"

I nodded at the boy. "Yeah, but no thanks to him and his friends."

She bowed her head to us. "I am terribly sorry for my brother's terrible behavior. If I had any idea he was stealing sheep I would have stopped him long ago."

I looked from the boy to the young woman. "So you two are siblings?"

She raised her head and her eyes twinkled as she met my gaze. "Yes. As children of Valtameri we both are your cousins."

My eyes widened. I pointed a shaking hand at her. "You. . .do you know where he is?"

The young woman tilted her head to one side. "I do, but are you not concerned with returning home? And my brother-" she half-turned and gestured to the young man who floated behind her, "-is eager to make his apologies to your people."

I glanced between them. "That's great, but I'd really like to meet your dad, this Calamari guy. I've got something I want to ask him."

"You do?" Roisin spoke up.

The young woman frowned. "I cannot allow that. My father would be furious if I brought a mortal to the palace."

I held up one of my glowing hands. "But I'm a cousin, remember? What's a little meeting between family?"

My cousin shook her head. "While we are related, not all who share our lineage are to be trusted."

I gestured to the dark world around us. "Seriously, what am I going to steal around here?"

She held up the pearls. "These are priceless to your people, but to us they are sacred beauty. Others before you have stolen them from the palace, and my father was forced to deal harsh justice to our cousins."

"But I just want to talk!" I insisted.

She dropped the pearls and shook her head. "It cannot be allowed."

I clasped my hands together and rung them in front of her. "There's got to be some sort of exception. Some way you'd trust me."

She turned away from me toward her brother. He floated closer to us as she pursed her lips. "We have spoken too much and you have come too close to the palace. We must take you back."

I balled my hands into fists at my sides and glared at her. "Then if you don't trust me who would you trust? Another full-blooded fae?"

The siblings faced us side-by-side one another. The young woman furrowed her brow. "Please do not judge me too harshly. I do not set the laws in my father's domain."

"So you're saying that's a 'yes?'" I persisted.

She nodded. "Yes, I would be allowed to show another fae to my father's palace."

I half-turned from her and crossed my arms over my chest. "You sound like the humans on the surface. They're just as paranoid as you are. If you guys had been the first fae

I met, or I-" My eyes widened. I snapped my fingers and turned to my fae cousins. "What if I could prove I'm a friend of the fae? Would you take us to the palace?"

She arched an eyebrow. "That would depend on what you have to show me."

I dug around in my pocket and drew out the soul stone given to me by Thorontur. Its faint green hue glowed in the darkness of the black water as I held it up for my cousins to behold. The young man's mouth dropped open.

The young woman's eyes widened at the stone before she looked to me with interested eyes. "You are very blessed, cousin. That is a most powerful stone."

"But will it get us an audience with your dad?" I asked her.

She smiled and gave a nod. "It will, and I apologize for not trusting you sooner."

I stuffed the soul stone back into my pocket and grinned. "I'll forgive you if you tell me one thing."

She arched an eyebrow. "What is it you wish to know?"

"Your name."

The young woman's face softened and her eyes smiled at me. She bowed her head. "My name is Aeronniell, but you may call me Niell." She raised her head to catch my gaze. "And what is your name, cousin?"

I held out my hand. "It's Miriam, daughter of-um, somebody."

Niell tilted her head to one side and studied me. "You do not know your father?"

I shook my head. "Nope, or my mom, but I'm hoping your dad can change that. Can we go see him right now?"

"Of course, but-" Niell glanced at Roisin, "-do you wish to return to the surface? My brother Aearion-" she gestured to the young man, "-would be glad to escort you."

Roisin shook her head. "I will not leave without you."

"Then please allow us to escort both of you," the fae woman requested.

My cousins turned and swam back in the direction they'd appeared. Roisin and I followed them. I looked to my friend and lowered my voice. "You really don't have to come with me if you don't want to."

She smiled and shook her head. "You are my friend, and a friend does not leave one another behind to face anyone, especially someone as great as Valtameri."

I arched an eyebrow. "So you know who he is?"

She nodded. "Yes. That is the name of the ancient god whom my people worshiped."

I whistled. "You had a pretty nice god watching over you. We'll have to ask him how come he went from being a benevolent god to letting his kids run amok with your sheep."

Roisin's eyes widened at me. "Oh no! We could never insult a god!"

I grinned. "Just watch me."

"But-"

"I'm family, remember?" I teased as we followed our guides.

The two fae led us deeper into the depths of darkness. A few hundred yards further into the bleak blackness the way began to lighten. Giant reefs of glowing white coral sprouted from the ocean floor some half mile beneath us and rose to a towering height over our heads. Their cylindrical bodies pulsed with a soft, warm light that lit up a path of thick green seaweed that wound through their forest. For the first time we saw other fae. They swam through the water like the fishes that scattered before our coming. Many stopped and stared at us. I felt like I was back in the city of the humans.

We followed the green path until the coral parted. Their light stretched far ahead of us, but in that space stood a tall, conch shell-shaped palace of white glistening stone. The rock was like quartz in that it reflected the bright light of the coral reefs. The edges of the palace were smoothed to a glistening shine that reflected the darkness and light that surrounded it. Four sets of open gates led into the shell palace.

Around the palace was a magnificent city made from the same white stone, but the walls of the buildings weren't as reflective as the palace. The layout was circular with bands of seaweed beds that partitioned the city into terrace-like blocks. Many of the residents gathered in talkative groups on the beds like they were roads.

I looked to Roisin. "I think I know where your people got the idea for their city." She could only nod as her eyes were glued to the scene.

Our guides directed us to one of the sets of open gates. My fae cousins floated down to the seaweed and stepped onto the green carpet. The seaweed gave a little under their weight, but bounced back and supported them. Roisin and I followed suit, and together the four of us walked through the towering gates and into the palace of the ocean god.

CHAPTER 24

The inside was no less reflective. I stared at myself through normal mirrors, and others that were more funhouse-like. "Does your dad like to look at himself?" I asked my cousins.

Niell shook her head. "Not exactly. He wishes for everyone to reflect on themselves, and in some instances-" she gestured to an exaggerated mirror image of herself that made her look skinny and fat, "-to laugh at one's self."

I leaned toward Roisin and lowered my voice to a whisper. "As if I wasn't funny enough." I cringed when my voice echoed around the wide halls.

Niell looked over her shoulder at me and smiled. "There are no secrets in the halls of my father, and I would never consider your handsome features to be repulsive in any light."

I rubbed the back of my head and sheepishly grinned. "Thanks, but you're just being nice."

She shook her head. "No, I speak the truth, and we are here."

A pair of white stone doors some twenty feet height stood at the end of the hall. Niell pushed them open and presented us with a view of a grand throne room. The design was circular like that of the humans, but there were no guards. Instead, citizens like those on the seaweed roads loitered along the walls. Their attention fell on us as we entered, but my attention was before us.

In the center of the room stood a tall platform. The pedestal was twice the size of the one that belonged to King Cathal, and the steps that led up to the top were twice as wide as I was tall. At the top of the steps was a large throne, and on that throne sat a towering man. His skin was of a bluish tint, and he sports a seaweed-like beard that traveled down his naked chest. He was clothed in seaweed shorts, but atop his green-haired head was a crown of coral.

The crowned man, who I assumed was Valtameri, had one elbow atop an arm of the throne and leaned his cheek against his balled hand. He raised his head as we entered.

Niell pushed off from the floor and landed well ahead of our party and close to the foot of the tall throne. She bowed her head. "Father, I have brought guests."

Valtameri arched an eyebrow as he looked at his daughter. "How did you come to meet them?"

Niell gestured to her brother who hung back with us. "Aearion found a way into the ancient pool and stole the sheep of the humans," the young woman explained. She nodded at Roisin and me. "They disguised themselves as sheep and were mistakenly taken into our realm."

Valtameri's heavy gaze fell on the quivering form of his son. "How did you find your way to the pool? The earthquake blocked the path long ago."

Aearion hung his head. "I found a narrow path through the rumble."

"And why did you steal the sheep?"

The young man shrank into himself. "I-it was a game, Father. We wished to see how many sheep we could capture without being caught by the humans."

His sister glared at him. "Have you no decency? Did you not think of the humans you were harming? Or the sheep?"

He raised his head and shook it. "We did not harm the sheep."

"Then where are they?" she questioned him.

He sheepishly grinned. "We placed them on the Goat Islands."

Her mouth dropped open. "But those are on the other side of the world! What did you expect to do with them there?"

He shrugged. "Let them have some fun with the goats?"

His sister opened her mouth, but a long, low chuckle interrupted her. All eyes fell on the stoic figure on the throne. Valtameri stroked his beard as he studied his son. A smile was partially hidden beneath the long, seaweed-like hair. "You sought to solve their population problem?"

Aearion grinned and nodded. "Yes!"

I stepped forward. "He solved one problem and made a whole bunch of new ones for humans *and* dragons."

Valtameri arched an eyebrow. "How so?"

I glanced over my shoulder at Roisin and smiled at her. "Now's your chance to really help your people."

Roisin shuffled to my side and lowered her eyes to the floor. "Y-Your Highness, o-our sheep provide us with-"

"Speak up, young one," Valtameri gently scolded her.

Roisin swallowed the lump in her throat and lifted her eyes to meet his chest. "My people need our sheep to provide us with food and clothing, and we trade them for other goods." Her voice grew louder. "Many people suffered. Without our sheep we had to invade the coast and attack dragons with whom we had had a long peace."

"And you would say that was your only choice?" he asked her.

She straightened and looked him in the eyes. Her eyebrows pushed down as she frowned at him. "Many of us prayed for guidance. I prayed to you, and received nothing but more stolen sheep."

I winced and leaned toward her where I lowered my voice to a whisper. "Whatever happened to not insulting gods?"

Valtameri leaned back in his throne and studied Roisin. His head slowly nodded. "You speak the truth, young one. I and my own have failed your people in many ways, and for that you have my sincerest apologies."

Roisin shook her head. "I cannot accept your apology, Your Highness. My people would rather have their sheep returned."

He chuckled. "And you shall have it, but not all at once. I shall have my sons return your sheep to you themselves, but that is not a quick task, and-" his eyes flickered to Aearion, "-I hope not easy. Meanwhile-" Valtameri reached into his skimpy shorts and drew out a small, smooth stone. He flicked the stone to Roisin who caught it in both hands and opened them. I leaned toward her and saw a small mark in the shape of a trident on the front of the stone. "Have your people mark their bows with my symbol, and they are guaranteed to have a bountiful harvest of fish," he assured her.

Roisin smiled and bowed her head. "Thank you, Your Highness. My people will be most pleased to hear they have your blessing once more."

Valtameri smiled. "And I will be glad to be among your people again after my son has made recompense." He turned his attention to me. "You have helped the humans much in their troubles, but I sense you have your own reason for coming here."

I nodded. "Yeah, I do. Beriadan told me you could tell me about myself like who my parents are."

He arched an eyebrow. "Can you not remember them?"

I shook my head. "No. I was really young when I was found in an alley."

He smiled. "Any age is old enough to have some memories."

I snorted. "If I did I've forgotten them."

Valtameri raised himself to his feet. His full glorious stature of nearly seven feet made dwarves of everyone else. I gawked at his formidable form as he floated from his high perch and landed in front of me. Roisin and Aearion instinctively stepped back, but I was mesmerized by his soft blue eyes.

Valtameri pushed his hand through my bubble without piercing it and set his palm over my forehead. His soft, soothing voice echoed around me. "Perhaps you need only a little help to remember them."

I gasped as a pleasant dampness penetrated my skull. A blinding flash of light swallowed the room, and when my vision returned I was somewhere else. The world was a blurry mess, but I could make out a ceiling above me. There were wooden walls on all four sides.

A baby cried. It took me a few moments to realize it was me. A shadow appeared over the walls. I could make out hair as black as mine, but the facial features were too blurry to see.

"What is the matter, Estelwen?" a soft male voice asked me as the person picked me up.

He cradled me against his chest and set a rattle in my hand. "We're going to see Mommy soon. Would you like that?" I heard my own cooing voice. He laughed. "I'm glad you feel the same way." He paused and looked ahead of him into the distance. His face fell and his smile slipped off his lips. "I just wish it was for a better reason."

Another flash of light blinded me. When I could open my eyes the scene had changed. Colors of green and blue mingled together. A bright blue light hovered over me. Smooth, warm hands picked me up and I was cradled against a cool, soothing body. The person rocked me back and forth.

"She has grown," a melodious woman's voice spoke up.

"She has, and one day she'll be as beautiful as her mother," the man replied.

The woman stopped rocking me. Her voice changed. There was tension in her words. "Have they learned?"

"No, but I believe he suspects that she is not my adopted daughter," the man answered.

"What will you do?"

The man moved into my vision and looked down at me. There was a dark aura around him that made me fuss. "I don't know, but I promise you that whatever happens she'll be safe."

The scene flashed to another one. This one was shrouded in night. The man's head was hidden by the hood of a dark cloak. His labored breathing and the breeze over me told me we were running. I could hear shouts from behind us. They were angry voices.

"Over here!"

"They went this way!"

"Quickly!"

I cried. I couldn't stop myself. I was terrified.

"They're over there!"

The man slid to a stop and cradled me in one arm. He thrust his other one out in front of him. A portal opened before us. Through the fuzzy doorway I could make out an alley. It was raining.

He raised me up and looked at me. I could see blurry tears stream down his face. "Goodbye, little Estelwen. May you live up to your name."

The man pressed a kiss on my forehead and threw off his cloak. He wrapped me tightly in the cloak and clasped me in both hands before he drew back his arms.

"Stop!" a voice yelled behind us.

The man tossed me forward and through the portal. I landed neatly on my back and faced the gateway. The man drew his hand across the portal and turned his back on me. The entrance began to shut. I saw a group of men confront the single man.

One of them stepped forward. In the dark I could make out red eyes. "You are more trouble than you are worth, human."

The other man scoffed. "Wait until my daughter returns."

The first man chuckled. "You will not live to see that day." He raised his hand and snapped his fingers.

The crowd behind him lunged at the man who saved me. They fell upon him just as the portal shut.

"Dad!"

I stretched out my hand. My foot stumbled on the stone floor of the ocean palace and I fell forward. Roisin caught my shoulders and slowed my fall so I crumpled to the ground. Tears stained my cheeks.

I cupped my face in my hands and sobbed. "He's dead. They killed him."

"Your father?" Roisin guessed.

I raised my head and nodded. "Yeah. He. . .he died saving me." I tilted my head back to look into the concerned face of the ocean king. "But why couldn't I remember his face? Or my mother's?"

He closed his eyes and shook his head. "A magic hangs over your memories and keeps them hidden from even my powers. It was cast with love, and nothing but one's own realization can break such powerful magic."

I climbed to my feet and wiped my nose with my sleeve before I gazed into the old eyes of Valtameri. "What does Estelwen mean?"

"Hope."

CHAPTER 25

Our business was finished, and so we were led by my cousins to the entrance to the pond. The bright night sky cast light into the surface above us as Roisin and I stopped and turned to our guides.

Niell clasped my hands and smiled at me. "It was an honor to meet you, Miriam."

I nodded. "Ditto." I glanced past her at Aearion. "Don't go stealing any more animals, all right?" He winced, but nodded.

I drew myself out of Niell's grasp and turned to Roisin. Her dragon wings were still out. "You going to go like that?" I asked her.

She smiled and nodded. "Yes."

I grinned and took hold of one of Roisin's hands. "Good."

Together we kicked our way to the surface and broke through the fine line between air and sky. The glittering stars greeted us with their cold light. A cool breeze swept over us and reminded us we were home.

"There they are!" came a shout.

The guards of the pond held torches, and the weak, flickering light of fire was cast upon us. Xander splashed into the water toward us. We met him halfway where our feet touched the bottom.

He grasped my upper arms and looked me over. His face was fraught with relief and fear. "Are you all right?"

I smiled and nodded. "Never better."

Spiros came up beside us with Cayden behind him. "What happened?"

I grinned. "It turns out my cousin the water god swiped the sheep as a game. They should be coming back any time now."

Roisin passed us and walked over to King Cathal. Her wings were folded behind her. The guards of the grove tensed. Some drew their swords and hurried to stand before their king.

Cathal raised his hand. His men froze behind him, but they still glared at Roisin.

Roisin knelt before her king and bowed her head. "Your Highness, the ocean god sends his apologies. Until the sheep are all returned he has promised a bountiful harvest of fish to any ship that bears his mark on its bow." She didn't raise her head as she opened her palm to his highness and revealed the tiny stone before she bowed her head.

The king took the stone and looked down on Roisin with a softened gaze. He cupped her chin and raised her astonished eyes to him. "Thank you, little daughter." Roisin's her mouth dropped open. Cathal smiled at her. "You have done your people proud."

"You're damn right!" I agreed.

Xander swept me into his arms and carried me toward shore. Spiros and Cayden followed, but we left the humans behind in their jubilant celebration. "I would like a more thorough explanation, if you would."

I wrapped my arms around his neck and smiled. "Sure thing, partner." I glanced over to Roisin. "You coming, too, partner?"

Roisin stood and turned to me with a smile. She shook her head. "Not at the moment. I must tell Mother that all is well."

I grinned. "Tell her Dreail still wants to see her if she changes her mind."

Roisin bowed to me. "I will, and thank you for everything."

I gave her a thumbs up. "No problem."

My new friend nodded and hurried past us toward the path. She unfurled her wings and flew into the sky.

King Cathal turned to us. He grasped the stone in one hand at his side. "If you would I would like to hear the details of your adventure."

I cringed and looked to Xander. "Do I have to?"

He smiled and nodded. "Yes."

We returned to the palace with the king and his entourage. I had new admiration for the architecture of the king's home, but it was nothing compared to the original.

One of the servants of the palace hurried up to us as we entered the entrance hall. He bowed to Cathal. "Your Highness, the red dragon has disappeared."

Cathal frowned. "How did this happen? I ordered him to be watched at all times."

The servant shook his head. "I cannot say, Your Highness, but he is not to be found."

Xander stepped forward. "I believe he has learned he cannot offer his 'help' and has left, Your Highness."

Cathal set his hand on the top of his sword and slowly nodded his head. "That is well. I did not like the look in his eyes. But come."

We had an audience with his highness in the throne room where I regaled everyone with my tales of watery adventures. I may have omitted a few minor personal details.

When I finished King Cathal leaned back in his throne and stroked his chin. A smile played across his lips. "I see. I am grateful for you for helping my people." He stood and bowed to Cayden. "As the god of the ocean has given his promise, I will give mine. My people will no longer raid your coasts, and as a sign of our new bond I will give you this." The king walked down the steps and untied the skull at his side. He stood before Cayden and held the skull out with both hands. "Please forgive my people for our desperate act."

Cayden smiled and shook his head. "There is nothing to forgive." He took the skull and bowed. "May this peace last many generations."

Cathal smirked. "Many of your generations, you mean."

Cayden chuckled. "Indeed."

I watched the true with a soft smile on my lips. A feeling made me glance at my left where stood Xander. His eyes studied me. I leaned away from him and frowned. "What?" I whispered. He closed his eyes and shook his head.

OCEANS BENEATH DRAGONS

I pursed my lips and turned my head away, but I stared at him out of the corners of my eyes. He looked ahead, but I still had the feeling his full attention was on me.

King Cathal stepped back and glanced around the entrance hall. "The night is growing short. We should rest and tomorrow we will return you to your ship."

Cayden bowed his head. "Thank you, Your Highness."

We made our bows and went to our rooms for a long rest. At least, that's what I planned. Xander and I shared a room, and I was the first one inside. It was a nice enough room with a sheep-theme down to the rug on the floor. The bed called to my weary limbs.

I stretched my arms above my head and smiled. "I feel like I could sleep for a million years." The door shut ominously behind me. I turned to find Xander standing in front of it staring at me. I raised an eyebrow. "What's with that face?"

"What did you omit from your retelling to the king?" he asked me.

I cringed. "That obvious, huh?" He nodded. My shoulders slumped and I turned away. "If you must know, I asked Valtameri about my folks."

Xander moved to stand just behind me. "What did you tell you?"

I pushed back the tears that sprang into my eyes. "He showed me some of my memories. I. . .I saw my dad die saving me."

Xander set his hands on my shoulders. "I am sorry."

A sad smile slipped onto my lips as I shook my head. "Don't be, I'm not. I mean, he was so cool at the end opening that portal and tossing me through." Xander started back and his hands gripped my shoulders tightly. I looked over my shoulder at him. His eyes were wide. "What? What's wrong?"

He gathered himself and frowned down at me. "You are sure he made a portal?"

I nodded. "Yeah. He threw out his hand and it just opened. Why? Is that against the law here?"

Xander nodded. "Yes. It is against the very laws that govern my world."

I arched an eyebrow. "But there's the Portal at the High Castle."

"There is, but that was created under the close guidance of some of the greatest sorcerers of the age. There was no fear of tearing apart the thin wall that separates our worlds," he told me.

I blinked at him. "'Tearing apart the thin wall?' What happens if that gets torn down?"

Xander pursed his lips and a dark shadow fell over his expression. "I am not sure. There are some who believe that would such a thing occur that both worlds would merge peacefully."

"And other people?"

"They believe it would end both worlds."

I cringed. "Maybe what my dad did wasn't such a good idea." An idea hit me. I straightened and furrowed my brow as I stared at the floor. "But if a bunch of powerful sorcerers made the Portal at the High Castle, how'd my dad make one just by waving his hand?"

Xander shook his head. "I do not know, but we may find the answer to that questions at that lies past Rimal Almawt al'Abyad in the Temple of the Priests of the Portal."

I raised an eyebrow. "Come again?"

OCEANS BENEATH DRAGONS

"Rimal Almawt al'Abyad means 'The Sands of White Death.' The temple of the priests, of which Apuleius is one, lies to the far south of its deadly white beauty."

My shoulders drooped and I hung my arms out in front of me. "So more danger?"

He set his hands on my shoulders and looked me in the eyes. "To find the truth is often a laborious task. I would not blame you if you remained in Alexandria-"

"Oh hell no." I knocked away his hands and crossed my arms over my chest. "I'm not being left behind, especially if it means finding out who my parents are, or were, or whatever, so you're stuck with me."

He smiled and leaned down to peck a gentle kiss on my lips. "I would have it no other way."

CHAPTER 26

The following day Cathal made good on his promise and led us back to the our away-boat. He turned to Cayden and bowed his head. "It was a pleasure to meet you, Dragon Lord."

Cayden smiled and returned the gesture. "And you as well, King of Ui Breasail."

Cathal raised his head and a sly grin slipped onto his lips. "It is almost a pity there is now a truce between us. I would have liked to have tested my blade against your skills."

Cayden shook his head. "I do not believe I would have liked the outcome."

The king chuckled. "Perhaps one day we will duel in a more settled time, but for now I wish you a speedy voyage."

"Wait!" We looked back toward the trees. Roisin appeared from the canopy flying at a great speed. In her arms was the small form of her mother. She landed them on the shore and rushed across the dock toward us. "Please wait!" Cathal's guards parted and Roisin slid to a stop in front of us. She breathed hard as she set her mother on the boards and bowed to us. "Please allow us to accompany you back to the mainland."

Cayden glanced at Mac Bradaigh. "You both wish to come?"

A crooked grin slid onto her wizened old lips. "I'd like to see the old geezer one last time so I can give him what he deserves."

Cayden chuckled. "I do not envy Dreail."

"Then you will take us?" Roisin asked him.

Cayden bowed his head. "Yes. That is, if your mother would consent to free my friend here-" he gestured to Xander, "-of the curse of the Dragon's Bane."

Mac Bradaigh reached into a pocket and drew out a vial which she wiggled in front of us. "I have enough for him and anyone else this fool-" she jerked her head toward Cathal, "-might have hurt."

Cathal blanched and stepped forward. "You intend to return, do you not?"

Mac Bradaigh shrugged as she tossed the vial to Xander who deftly caught it in one hand. "Perhaps, perhaps not, but if you're worried about the Bane you'll find enough in my cottage to last a long while. That is, if you don't go wasting it like you have."

Cathal bowed his head. "Thank you for your kindness, Mac Bradaigh."

She waved him away. "Don't thank me, thank my daughter. She's the one who thought you might need it."

The king smiled at the dragon girl. "On behalf of our people I thank you, young Roisin."

She blushed and shook her head. "It was my pleasure, Your Highness."

"Now let us be off," Cayden called out.

We boarded the away-boat and rowed to the vessel outside the bay. The crew was eager to see us, and after much joyful exchanges we set sail.

I walked up to Xander as he stood at the bow. He held the vial in his hand and stared down at it. "Tried it yet?" I asked him as I leaned against the railing.

He nodded. "Yes, and I feel no different."

I frowned. "She said it'd work."

Xander pocketed the vial and swept me into his arms. I blinked up at him as he used a crate to step up onto the railing. The rough seas below us crashed into the sharp bow of the ship.

I whipped head up to stare into his impassive face. "What are you doing?"

"I am nothing without my strength, and if I cannot protect you then I will take you with me," he replied.

My eyes widened. "No! Xander, don't you-" He leaned forward.

We fell into the abyss between life and death. I screamed and clutched onto his neck. The waves came up on us. I shut my eyes and awaited splashdown.

It didn't come. There was a whoosh of wind and a little splattering of water. I peeked open an eye. The sea was far below us as we flew up toward the sun. I whipped my head up. Xander's wings were spread out behind him. He sported a devilish grin.

OCEANS BENEATH DRAGONS

I snarled at him and beat his chest with my fists. "You little liar! Don't do that again! You nearly scared me to death!"

He chuckled as he flapped his long wings. "I could not resist a bit of fun after you left me for your ocean people."

I crossed my arms and sank into his. "You could've just scolded me. . ."

"I thought perhaps you experiencing the same fear would be a better lesson."

I snorted. "I wasn't trying to kill myself, or you, for that matter."

He drew himself into a glide and looked down at me with a soft look. "If you were to die, then I would die."

I arched an eyebrow. "We're not connected that way, remember?"

He nodded. "I do, but you are my life. If. .. If I were to lose you I would not see life as worth living."

I turned my face away and pursed my lips. The wind blew over me and drew my hair behind me. The beautiful, endless expanse of water was like a long life without purpose. I sighed. "Well, I guess I can try a little harder to stay out of trouble, but only if you do, too."

Xander chuckled. "We will both try our best-"

I glanced back at him and smirked. "-and both fail epically."

"But together," he added.

I leaned forward and pecked a kiss on his lips. "Together."

CHAPTER 27

We reached land and the beautiful waters of the Bay of Secrets. A crowd waited for us as we landed on the long dock. Stephanie and Darda were at the head of the people.

Cayden stepped out of the away-boat and swept Stephanie into his arms. He hugged her close and then drew them to arm's length so he could see her belly. "Are you both well?"

She smiled and nodded. "Very well, but you-" she cupped his cheek in one hand, "-you look tired."

He grasped her hand and pressed a light kiss to her palm. "I will be better now that I have returned to you."

Darda moved to stand before us and bowed her head. "I am glad to see you returned, My Lord and Lady."

I playfully rapt my knuckle on the top of her head. "It's Miriam."

She raised her head and smiled. "You might indulge me some formality on your return, young Miriam."

I grinned and shook my head. "Nope."

"Has anything occurred while we were away?" Xander asked her.

She shook her head. "No, Xander. The area has been as quiet as the bay."

"Good, then we shall liven the beach with some gaiety tonight." He raised his arms above his head and raised his voice. "May I have your attention!" The dock quieted and all eyes turned to him. "There shall be a celebration tonight to mark the peace. Everyone is invited and food shall be provided!"

A great cheer arose from the crowd. Xander returned his attention to Darda. "If you would-"

"-handle the affairs," she finished for him as she bowed her head. "With pleasure."

"This is the mainland?" Roisin's voice spoke up behind me.

I turned around and smiled at her as I held out my hand. "This is just the start. It goes for a really long time."

She returned my smile with one of her own as she took my hand. "Then lead me as far as you may, my friend Miriam."

I drew her down the dock with her mother close behind us. We reached the end where the planks met the sand. The crowds parted as everyone hurried to prepare for the magnificent feast that was to being in only a few short hours.

"Caoimhe." Our group turned in the direction of the voice. Dreail stood on the beach to the left of the dock. His wide eyes gazed at Mac Bradaigh in wonder. He took a step forward and stretched out a wrinkled, shaking hand. "Is that truly you?"

Mac Bradaigh eyebrows crashed down. She rolled up her sleeves, marched up to him, and gave a nice right hook into his left cheek. The old man stumbled back and tripped over sand. He landed with a soft thud on the beach while she towered over him with her fists on her hips.

"Is that all you've got to say to me after all these years? And not even asking about your daughter?" she growled.

His eyes bulged. "D-daughter."

Mac Bradaigh half-turned and gestured to Roisin. The young dragon girl stared in wonder and curiosity at Dreail. The old man's mouth dropped to the sand.

Roisin smiled and leaned down to offer her hand to him. "It is a pleasure to meet you, Father."

Dreail's mouth flopped like a gasping fish. He turned his attention to Mac Bradaigh and pointed at Roisin. "She's. . .she's really mine?"

Mac Bradaigh nodded. "Yes, and don't just standing there gaping. Get up!"

Dreail swallowed the lump in his throat and returned his attention to Roisin. He stretched out his shaking hand and grasped hers. She pulled him to his feet and leapt at him, enveloping him in a tight hug.

"I am so happy to meet you, Father!" she exclaimed.

Dreail hesitated before he wrapped his arms around her. A soft smile graced his lips as he closed his eyes. "And I with you, Daughter."

"Her name's Roisin," Mac Bradaigh told him.

Dreail chuckled and parted them, but left his arm draped over Roisin's shoulders as he looked to Mac Bradaigh. "Is she? That suits her. A rose for a thorny family."

"Who's thorny you old crab?" Mac Bradaigh growled.

Dreail drew Roisin over to her mother so he could loop his free arm around her waist. His eyes twinkled as he studied her wizened old face. "That's my spirited lady. Now come along with ya and tell me what you've been up to." He drew them away from us, but paused and glanced over his shoulder at our group. Dreail bowed his head to Cayden. "Thank you, My Lord, for bringing me a family."

Cayden smiled and returned the bow. "Your happiness is thanks enough."

The old man winked. "I don't know about that, but ya can be sure of a good feast of fish tonight, My Lord."

The three of them walked down the beach together. Xander looped his arm around my waist and smiled down at me. "Let us now rest before the party."

We made our way to Cayden's chateau. The liveliness of the party preparations meant there was very little rest, but a lot of fun. Food streamed through the house and out onto the beach where the local guard, now cured of the affliction of the Dragon's Bane, set up tables and chairs that stretched down the white sands. They staked tall, unlit torches around the area in preparation for night.

As evening arrived the residences of the other chateaus emerged with more food. A long line of the locals moved down the road from the interior laden with fruit and vegetable goods. I stood on the deck out back and saw Colin arrive with his mother and father. He waved to me. I smiled and waved back.

The commotion was wonderful. People talked and laughed. The tables groaned under the weight of the good food. Night came and the guard lit the torches, creating halos of light that cast long shadows over the smiling faces. A bonfire was erected close to the edge of the water, and people danced in time with music played by local flutists who had made their instruments from the reeds of the ocean.

I stood between Xander and Cayden some twenty feet from the bonfire. A light tap on my shoulder made me turn around. Lady Abha stood behind me. A soft smile graced her lips. "I see you have been much growing since we last met."

I grinned and shrugged. "Just a little. I learned the Call."

She chuckled. "Then you are a step closer to realizing who you truly are."

I arched an eyebrow. "What do you-"

"My Lord! Lord Cayden!" a voice shouted. The music died down as Colin's father hurried up to us. He was out of breath as he bowed his head to Cayden. "My Lord, you must help my wife and me! We cannot find our son!"

Cayden looked softly at his subject as he set a hand on the man's shoulder. "We will all help with the search." He swept his eyes over everyone present. "Pull the torches from the sand and form parties of ten! Search from the waves to the forest!"

There was a ruckus of organization as people placed themselves in groups as instructed. The torches were pulled up and each given to the leader of the group. Other torches were brought from the chateaus and farm houses, and soon the celebrators parted for the search.

Xander took a torch and turned to Stephanie and me. "Please search the chateaus. We will search the bay."

I glared at him. "Why can't we go with-" He unfurled his wings, as did the other dragons. My face fell. "Oh. That's why."

OCEANS BENEATH DRAGONS

The dragon men flew into the sky and disappeared in the direction of the barracks. I turned to Stephanie. Her face was tense. "That poor boy. He must be so scared."

I set my hands on her shoulders and drew her toward the large houses. "He's probably out blowing that whistle Xander. . .gave to. . .him."

Stephanie blinked at me. "Are you okay?"

I stopped and furrowed my brow. "I think I might know where he is."

"Where?"

I grabbed her hand and tugged her down the beach. "Come on!"

CHAPTER 28

We rushed across the sand. The search parties scoured the beach and the high road, but I noticed they avoided the left-hand cliffs of the calm bay. The rumors of the ghostly lady kept them far from that cursed place.

Stephanie and I reached the edge and found a wind-worn set of stone steps like those on the opposite side. We climbed the stairs and, though winded, made it to the top. The darkness of the night was made darker by a light layer of clouds above us.

I leaned forward and squinted my eyes. "We should've brought a flashlight or something." A soft, shrill whistle caught my attention. I whipped my head to Stephanie. Her wide eyes told me she'd heard it, too. "Come on."

OCEANS BENEATH DRAGONS

I led the way across the cliffs. The rough water of the ocean crashed against the other side and splashed droplets of water at our feet. Puddles dotted the rocky top.

We were a hundred feet from the end of the cliff when I spotted shadows. One piggish-snouted one was familiar. It was the sus from before, the one who'd watched me on the beach as I handled my Soul Stone. Two dragon men with their wings unfurled stood on either side of him. One of them held Colin by the shoulders. The lad's arms were pinned to his sides by rope and his wings were pinned to his back.

Stephanie and I made it to within ten feet of them before the sus's deep voice rang out across the cliffs. "That's close enough."

I stopped and glared at him. "Let him go."

"Help me!" Colin yelled.

"It'll be all right," I told him.

The sus held out his hand. "Only if you hand over that Soul Stone."

"I don't have it on me," I lied.

He chuckled and shook his head. "You're a terrible liar, now hand it over or-" He nodded at his henchman.

The dragon man lifted Colin into the air and turned to face the ocean side of the cliffs. Colin squirmed. "Help! Please help me!"

"Stop!" I shouted.

The sus stretched his hand closer to me. "Only if you give me the stone."

I pursed my lips, but reached into my pocket and drew out the stone. The Soul Stone pulsed with its green light. I nodded at Colin. "Set him down." The sus nodded at the dragon man who set Colin back on the ground. "Now untie him."

The sus shook his head. "I can't do that. The little boy might fly away, and then my plan would be ruined."

"You can't get away, anyway. We're on a cliff, remember?" I pointed out.

My foe grinned. "I've got a boat waiting for me, but that's none of your business. Now hand over the stone."

"First the boy."

"The stone, or the boy learns he can't float in the ocean."

I pursed my lips and gripped the stone tightly in my hand. Colin shook as he stared pleadingly at me. I sighed and marched toward them. One of my heavy feet stepped into a puddle and water splashed onto my hand. I felt something squirm in my palm that held the stone. An idea struck me.

I stopped five feet from the group and I held up the stone. "You want this? Then catch it."

I tossed the stone into the air. The sus and his men watched the arc like birds watching a shiny object. I knelt and scooped up a handful of water. A small dragon formed from my hand as the stone started its downward fall.

The sus caught the stone as I cupped my hands together and stretched out my arms in front of me. "I hope you like getting wet!"

My foes returned their attention to me as my dragon, now twice the size, drew itself from my hand and lunged at them. Its wet, snapping jaws wrapped around the head of the dragon who held Colin. His scream was garbled by the water. He released the boy and tried to grab the water dragon, but he couldn't get a grip on the water.

OCEANS BENEATH DRAGONS

Colin stumbled toward us, but tripped on a stone. Stephanie rushed forward and caught him. "Get back!" I shouted at her.

She nodded and led the young boy away. I returned my attention to the sus and his henchman. One dragon man was still trapped in my watery prison, but the sus stepped back with a grin on his face. He tossed the whistle onto the ground and raised his arms.

"It was a pleasure doing business with you," he called out as the freed dragon man flapped into the sky and grabbed his boss's hands.

Together the pair flew into the sky. I pulled my dragon off the abandoned man who collapsed unconscious to the ground and turned the watery fury on them. My dragon stretched itself to the limit, but its jaws missed the sus's heels by half an inch. I rushed to where they stood and glared up at their disappearing figures above me.

My foot kicked something. I looked down. The whistle. I grinned and picked up the instrument. There was a theory I had to try out. I took a deep breath and blew.

The sharp whistle blew across the calm bay waters and echoed against the opposite cliff. It wasn't a moment later that two groups of dragon men, one made up of the guards and the other with Xander in the lead, flew in my direction. They aimed for me.

I pointed at the sus and dragon man who flew across the ocean. "Get them!"

The guards and Xander's group turned toward the sus and his henchman. The dragon man, seeing their pursuers, promptly dropped his heavy load. The sus's scream reached me.

Fortunately for him, the guards were fast. Two of them swooped down and caught each of his arms. The dragon henchman couldn't match the speed of Spiros, and was duly caught. They were flown back and dropped at my feet. The sus looked up at me and shrank back.

I knelt in front of him and held out my hand. "Give it."

He reluctantly dropped the Soul Stone into my palm. I stood and turned to Xander as he landed neatly near me. I held up his whistle and grinned. "You have to make me one of these."

He strode over and wrapped me tightly in his arms. His twinkling eyes looked down on me with a teasing light. "Will trouble never cease to follow you?"

I shook my head. "Nope, but about that whistle-"

Xander reached into his shirt and drew out a small whistle exactly the size as the other one, but made from the local driftwood. "Only if you say please."

I rolled my eyes. "Pretty please?"

"Miriam." I glanced at Stephanie.

Colin stood in front of her with his ropes gone. He rushed over and hugged my legs. "You saved me!"

I stooped and smiled as I held out his whistle. "Your whistle saved you, so keep good care of it, okay?"

He took the whistle and nodded. "I will!"

"Colin! Colin!" We looked down the cliff and watched his parents fly up to us. They embraced him in a tight family hug before his mother looked over at me.

"Thank you," she whispered.

I smiled and shrugged. "It was nothing." I looked up at Xander as he stood beside me. "So with everything closed here we're off to our next adventure, right?"

He smiled down at me and nodded. "Always."

A note from Mac

Thank you for purchasing my book! Your support means a lot to me, and I'm grateful to have the opportunity to entertain you with my stories.

If you'd like to continue reading the series, or wonder what else I might have up my writer's sleeve, feel free to check out my website at *macflynn.com*, or contact me at mac@macflynn.com.

* * *

Want to get an email when the next book is released? Sign up for the Wolf Den, the online newsletter with a bite, at *eepurl.com/tm-vn*!

Continue the adventure

Now that you've finished the book, feel free to check out my website at **macflynn.com** for the rest of the exciting series.

Here's also a little sneak-peek at the next book:

Deserts of the Dragons:

> The beautiful sky above me. The green forest and fields below me. A handsome dragon lord behind me. Everything was perfect.
> Well, almost perfect.
> "Do we have to fly all the way to the desert!" I yelped. Xander winced. My arms were wrapped tightly around his neck and my body was pressed close against his chest. "You did not wish to ride," he reminded me.
> I glared at him. "I have a tender bottom, okay? It wouldn't have taken a two-week trip. Besides-" I leaned back and admired his chest, "-not all the view is a terrifying death."
> Xander smiled. "I am glad I could be of service."
> I caught a peek over my shoulder at the woods far below us. They were the outlying forest of Thorontur, King of the Arbor Fae. There was also a little bit of green plains that represented Xander's dragon territory.

I cringed and looked back up into Xander's face. "You know, have you ever thought about bringing over a plane or car from my old world?"
Xander shook his head. "It is forbidden to bring any mechanical devices through the Portal."
My eyes narrowed at him. "What about that truck that drove me over?"
"That is an exception."
"Uh-huh. How about we make another teensy-weensy exception and I get a private jet?"
He blinked at me. "A 'jet?'"
I rolled my eyes and settled into his arms with my own crossed over my chest. "Never mind. So where are we going again?"
"To the outpost city of Almukhafar where we will travel by land over the desert to the Temple of the Priests of the Portal."
I arched an eyebrow. "Why don't we just fly across the desert?"
"You just expressed dissatisfaction in flying."
I shrugged. "Yeah, but I hate sand in my shoes more than I hate heights."
Xander looked ahead and pursed his lips. "The wings of dragons are incapable of withstanding the heat of Rimal Almawt al'Abyad. From Almukhafar we must travel by beast of burden to the Temple. Fortunately, it is only a journey of three days."
I cringed and rubbed my posterior. "Goodbye, soft butt cheeks."
He slyly grinned at me. "I might offer to massage them for you."
I snorted. "And I might take you up on that offer."
Spiros flew up beside us. His eyes twinkled with mischief. "I will gladly do my part to bring you comfort, My Lady, and offer to massage one of your cheeks."

"Captain Spiros!" Darda scolded him as she flew up behind we three.

"I will be the comfort for my Maiden," Xander assured him.

I raised an eyebrow at my dragon lord. "Don't I get a say in this?"

"No."

My eyes narrowed. "Listen, partner, on the rest of this steerage-class trip I will be the only one to massage my derriere."

Xander lifted his head and looked out over the horizon. A small smile crept onto his lips. "There is no need for that."

"Why?"

"Because we have arrived."

I whipped my head around to face forward. The green horizon abruptly stopped, and beyond the straight line was an endless stretch of white. The midday day sun illuminated the white sands and created a near-blinding display of light.

I blinked hard against the brilliance. "Please tell me you guys have invented sun glasses."

Xander chuckled. "There are special shades we may purchase in Almukhafar."

We flew the few short miles to the vast expanse of sand and touched down on the edge of a small city. The small metropolis was laid out in a grid pattern with narrow dirt streets between large blocks of buildings. Most of the city lay in the green grass of the straggling plains, but a few blocks stretched into the desert. The structures closest to us were built from the trees of Thorontur and rose two stories over the grassy plains. The houses in the desert were simple single-story buildings made of mud bricks.

People crowded the streets. Their skin was the color of soft brown maple leaves in the fall, and their attire was light and airy to handle the hot winds that blew off the desert. Many wore broad-brimmed hats of dried grass and carried fans of wood to cool themselves.

Many peddlers pushed narrow carts through the streets and shouted their wares to passers by.

"Fish! Get your fish! Caught in Alexandria only five days ago!"

"Pots! Pans! All that you could ever desire!"

"I have here the finest merchandise this side of the Potami. On sale today! Do not miss what I have to offer!"

Xander grasped my hand and smiled down at me. "Shall we?"

I grinned. "Let's do this."

We joined the throngs of people in the streets with Darda and Spiros at our backs. I was hit by a variety of pleasant smells that bespoke spicy food and roasted meat. Other smells weren't pleasant, and I found out what those were when someone leaned out an open second-floor window. They placed a pot on the sill and tipped it. The contents of a day's worth of waste dropped splattered onto the streets.

I cringed and pressed closer to Xander. "Lovely place. Remind me to book a vacation house sometime."

Xander swept his eyes over the area. "Do not think the less of the city. The outpost of Almukhafar is a very ancient city that has found it difficult to change some of its ways."

"Anything else I should be worried about?" I wondered.

He pursed his lips. "One cannot be too careful in such a place. There are many foreign travelers, and a simple matter of murder could be overlooked."

I felt the color drain from my face. "M-murder?"

Xander smiled down at me. "Do you believe I or any of us would allow such a fate to befall you?"

Spiros glanced to our right. The ground floor of some of the buildings opened into shops and taverns. Some unscrupulous characters leered at me. The captain laid his hand on the hilt of his sword and the men looked away.

I frowned at Xander. "I can protect myself, too. You're not the only dragon I've got, remember?"

"Your water abilities are limited here," he pointed out. I looked around. There wasn't a drop of liquid. My shoulders fell. "What I wouldn't do for a fire hydrant. . ."

Darda set a hand on my shoulder and smiled at me. "Let us pray to the gods you will not need our protection."

We reached a large square. Stalls were set up around the perimeter, and in the center was a large well. The vendors sold everything imaginable. Fruits, vegetables, animals of various sizes from mice to horses. Spices hung from long ropes, and tradesman advertised their clothing on thick pieces of wood.

The local women in their brightly-colored garb gathered around the well to exchange gossip. Men bartered and haggled at the stalls. Apprentices and shop boys scurried to and fro with delivery bundles under their arms.

"My Lord! Miriam!" The familiar voice came from the thick crowd of women gathered around the well, and soon a familiar sus emerged. It was Tillit. He strode over to us with his usual sly smile on his lips. Tillit took one of my hands in his and pecked a light kiss on the back of my hand before he raised his eyes to mine. "Might I saw you have grown lovelier than last I saw you, My Lady." Xander cleared his throat.

Tillit released my hand and straightened. "Have you only just arrived?"

"We have, but we do not intend to stay long," Xander told him.

The sus looked from me to Xander and back. "Looks like I caught you just in time. You're headed for the Temple, right?"

Xander nodded. "We are, but what brings you to the Temple? I was not aware you traded in pilgrimage goods."

Tillit snorted and waved a hand at Xander. "I've never touched the stuff, especially around that place. You can never tell when a dissatisfied customer would come back asking for a-" he paused and shuddered, "-refund."

"What are pilgrimage goods?" I spoke up.

The sus jerked his head over his shoulder at a line of six stalls. They all sold small figurines of naked women in dervish-style poses or seated like a Buddha. The women wore wreaths of grass around their heads and their expressions were friendly.

"Those are statues of the Alumu Aleazima, or Great Mother for those who don't speak Altinin," he told me. "She's the protector of merchants and desert wanderers, so you can see why she's so popular around here."

I swept my eyes over the busy trading area. "Why are there so many merchants this close to the desert?"

"Almukhafar is the last city before the desert, but beyond the sands in the southern part of the continent are many ports," Xander told me.

"And there's also the Temple," Tillit reminded him. "They run a pretty good business supplying the pilgrims who go there looking for the blessing of Alumu Aleazima and to get a look at some of those books in that library the priests have." His eyes

flickered to Xander. "But I'm sure you're not here to be bamboozled out of some of your gold, My Lord. Did something north of here get you down here?"
Xander arched an eyebrow. "You are referring to the incident at Bear Bay?"
I blinked at them. "Bear Bay?"
Tillit grinned. "Nothing gets past you, does it, My Lord? Anyway, you're right. I was there when it happened, and it's left me with a couple of questions I want answered."
"Such as?"
"What happened at Bear Bay?" I asked them.
The sus glanced around before he lowered his voice and leaned toward us. "Such as how a human was able to get into our world without using the Portal."
Xander frowned. Tillit studied him. "You look like you've heard this before, but not from Bear Bay."
"What happened?" I spoke up.
"Tell us what you can," Xander ordered him.
Tillit grinned and jerked his head down a narrow alley. "If you'll just step into my shop I'll answer both your questions."

Other series by Mac Flynn

Contemporary Romance
Being Me
Billionaire Seeking Bride
The Family Business
Loving Places
PALE Series
Trapped In Temptation

Demon Romance
Ensnare: The Librarian's Lover
Ensnare: The Passenger's Pleasure
Incubus Among Us
Lovers of Legend
Office Duties
Sensual Sweets
Unnatural Lover

Dragon Romance
Maiden to the Dragon

Ghost Romance
Phantom Touch

Vampire Romance
Blood Thief
Blood Treasure
Vampire Dead-tective
Vampire Soul

Werewolf Romance
Alpha Blood
Alpha Mated
Beast Billionaire
By My Light
Desired By the Wolf
Falling For A Wolf
Garden of the Wolf
Highland Moon
In the Loup
Luna Proxy
Marked By the Wolf
Moon Chosen
Continued on next page
Moon Lovers
Oracle of Spirits
Scent of Scotland: Lord of Moray
Shadow of the Moon
Sweet & Sour
Wolf Lake

Manufactured by Amazon.ca
Bolton, ON